I0667199

MATCHED WITH HER BROTHER'S BEST FRIEND

ROMANCE BY LOVE, AUSTEN
BOOK 5

BRITNEY M. MILLS

OPAL INK PUBLISHING

Copyright © 2024 by Britney M Mills

Cover design by Melody Jeffries

All rights reserved.

No part of this book may be reproduced in any form or by any electronic or mechanical means, including information storage and retrieval systems, without written permission from the author, except for the use of brief quotations in a book review.

To all my readers
Thank you for the encouragement to conquer my fears of
imperfection in these stories. You're my people.

1

MILLIE

It's official. I'm never watching kids again, at least until the panic from tonight's adventures wears off. After being a nanny for four years and practically raising my younger brothers, I thought I'd seen everything. But I've never lost a child in his own home. Yeah, the eight-year-old I'd sent to bed who wasn't there when I checked on him thirty minutes later. After an hour of searching, it turns out he'd cuddled up under the covers and I'd mistaken him for a pillow.

In the process, I stepped on at least four Legos, and my foot still aches as I walk down the street from the family's house to mine. I tuck a section of hair behind my ear and feel something cool and wet. Please don't let it be a slug or a worm or anything.

After a couple of steps and some quick breaths in and out, I reach up to touch it again, pull out a few strands of hair along with the substance. Oh good. Slime. Neon orange. How it got there, I have no idea.

I've been doing some babysitting on the side when I'm not studying for my college courses and it hasn't been as bad as the last family I nannied for a few months ago. Any bit of money helps keep me alive, as in potatoes and ramen, but I might need to get a job that's a little more normal. Boring even.

Okay, it's not that bad. I've learned from experience to scrimp for situations when money isn't coming in regularly, but it's still hard to spend any when I don't know what the future looks like. I've just switched from a graphic design major to studying business, but while studying, I make zero money.

I open the front door and stumble in, grateful that someone left the light on at midnight. That someone could only be a couple of people these days, since it seems like the roommates are all pairing up and getting married. Rachelle and then Dani. Kenzie is getting married this summer, but Evie's is just a month away.

Then it will be me and Hillary in the house. And that thought terrifies me.

She's intense and uber sarcastic, which I don't always catch onto. We've had a few conversations that went okay. Mostly if she can have some of my food, which I always say yes to. I don't need to be stabbed in my sleep. Would she actually do that? I don't know. I'm the second oldest of six kids, all brothers, so I'm mentally wired for the sabotage game.

I open the door and pull out my half gallon of milk. There isn't much in it, so I drain the rest and put the bottle into the recycling bin.

"You're back," a voice says behind me and I jump.

"Yep," I say, pasting a smile to Hillary.

"How was babysitting the brats?"

I blink a few times and then say, "One kid this time. I lost him for a bit, but at least I found him before the parents got home."

"Do you like kids that much?" Hillary asks, pulling out a mug and filling it with water from the sink. After it goes in the microwave, she pulls out a packet of herbal tea. That surprises me about her. I picture her more with the harder stuff, like the coffee that takes five minutes to explain to the barista, or shots of alcohol.

I shrug, leaning up against the counter. I'm not sure how long this conversation will be. Committing to sitting at the table with Hillary could be a severely bad idea, especially this late at night.

"I grew up practically raising my siblings. Taking care of someone else's kids can be harder sometimes, but at least I know it will end at some point. Then again, I'm ready for a career change. Do you have any openings at your job?"

Hillary grins. "If you're hoping to avoid kids, my line of work is not for you. Is that what brought you to Boston?"

"What?"

"Escape?"

I mull that over for a few moments and then nod. "I've never thought of it that way, but kind of. I needed out of my small town and all the responsibilities there. Since my brother always talked about the city, I figured this would be the place to start nannying while I figured out what I should do next."

I won't mention that I'd once overheard my long-time crush say that he could never be with anyone who hadn't traveled outside my hometown at least a few times. People tend to grow up in Bitter Springs and stick around, starting their own families without experiencing the world. I've only been to Boston, and the states between here and Bitter Springs, Colorado, since I drive back and forth when I go visit my family. World traveler I'm not, but at least I've been able to experience a bit more than if I'd stayed home. And I could at least check that off if Jordan Dietrich was to ever ask.

"So, are you planning on finding a man and settling down with a litter?" Hillary's eyes narrow in on my face and my hands fidget as I glance around the room. The microwave beeps, which helps give me a few seconds to come up with an answer.

How did she know I was thinking about Jordan? Okay, well,

her question wasn't as direct, but I still need to be better at keeping those emotions off my face.

"I mean, I hope to have a family someday, but I think I'm good to wait a while." And then, as I bravely continue the conversation and say, "What about you? Any plans to settle down?"

Hillary shoots me a death glare before she plops the tea bag into the mug. "You haven't heard the talk?"

I scrunch my forehead and shake my head. "I'm not sure what you mean."

"I left my fiancé at the altar."

"Really?" I'm not sure how I've lived under the same roof as Hillary this long and missed something like that.

She nods and settles into her chair. "Really. Roy was the guy my parents wanted me to marry, but when it was time to get the dress on and start a life with him, I panicked. And now I wish I could forget about the year after."

I should run, save myself from whatever is going to happen, but I can't bring myself to walk away, like I'm watching a train wreck in process.

"So, what happened after you left?" I avoid making eye contact by glancing at my cracked cell phone. I'll probably be able to replace it in the year 2075 at the rate I'm going with expenses.

Hillary lets out a long breath and says, "I ran off with some friends who I'd known for a while to an island and we had fun for a couple weeks. And then they left me there. I had no money and basically had to work as a pirate guide to get home."

I involuntarily laugh, trying to picture her in a pirate costume. For what?

But then I see that she's serious and I try to tamp down the laughter.

"It's all right. You're allowed to laugh at something as

ridiculous as that. I still can't believe it happened. I guess that spurred on the idea to dress up like a princess for kid parties."

I'd seen her a few times in large ball gowns or with wigs on to look like popular princesses, but I'd never taken the time to ask her why or how she got into that line of work. Because until now, we'd never talked this long.

"Do you like doing that? Dressing up, I mean."

She stares at me for several moments and finally nods. "Yeah, it helps pay the bills."

"I know how that goes. At least your sister is the owner of this house. I just don't want to get kicked out if I can't pay rent."

Hillary waves me off. "Rachelle would give you a grace period, and then she'd start trying to find you a job or giving you odd jobs around the house just to help you pay the rent. I wouldn't worry about it."

That thought surprises me. I moved in just a few weeks after Rachelle started dating her now husband Landon, so I never really knew her. But I'll do everything I can to owe no one, or as little as I can. My father is the king of negotiating until he gets a deal, and I always hated that scummy feeling of taking advantage of people.

"Where did you live before here?" Hillary asks.

"In an apartment with three other women. It was miserable."

Hillary nods and says, "In a small space, that's a recipe for disaster. Where are you from?"

"Bitter Springs, Colorado. It's a tiny town on the northeastern corner."

"Are you scared of me, Millie?" Hillary asks, leaning forward. I didn't even know she knew my name.

"A bit," I admit.

Hillary smiles and then laughs. "That's probably for the best. Everything I touch tends to die."

I don't have time to school my expression of horror before she says, "Not literally. I'm not a serial killer."

I let out a small laugh and stand, taking the bowl with me. "It was great to have this chat, but I have some homework calling my name."

My phone rings and I see it's Spencer, my brother's best friend. He's also good friends with the guys my roommates are dating or married to. Hillary must see it too.

"When are you two going to get together?"

I frown and gesture at my phone. "Me and Spencer? Yeah, that's not going to happen. He's like a brother." Sure, we've texted and talked a lot, and we do things together, a little more since Beau headed home to fix some things. But there's always the memory of Jordan. I have three significant memories that I replay in my mind daily about him.

The time he helped me pick up a large stack of papers and books after someone bumped into me in the hall and everyone kept walking past.

Another time when he helped me back up my car after I slid into a snowbank just after I got my driver's license.

And the time he asked me to dance at one of the school dances when I was all by myself.

Maybe once I'm done with school, I can go back and he'll see how different I am.

"Not from my angle. You guys are a lot closer than siblings." She stands and heads out of the room. I slump back down into my chair and swipe to answer the call, still confused by her words.

"Millie, what are you up to?" Spencer asks.

"I'm eating a midnight snack and just got done talking to Hillary."

There's a long pause on the other line before he speaks again. "Hillary talks to people? Are you all right?"

I shake my head and say, "I'm just as surprised as you are

about it. What are you doing up this late? I thought you were going to bed three hours ago."

"Yeah, I got sucked into a documentary and just finished. What are your plans for tomorrow?"

"Studying. What about you?"

"Wondering where your brother is. You haven't talked to him lately, have you?"

Beau isn't always aware of how his actions affect other people. The world revolves around him, or so he thinks.

"I haven't heard from him. I thought he'd be back by now." Beau had gone back to Bitter Springs two months ago to help our dad with some things at work, which was a shock, since Beau avoids any work like the plague.

"Me too. We're ready to launch the podcast and then I just have a couple other tweaks for the audio platform before that's ready."

"This is how Beau operates, though. He'll probably call soon and act like there's nothing wrong."

"True." There's a long pause before Spencer says, "There's an old film festival at the theater close to me. Do you want to join me next week? Jack doesn't like any shows or movies in black and white and well, Beau has been gone for a couple weeks. P-p-please Millie?" I try to picture Spencer's other best friend, Jack, watch old movies. He'd probably be making sarcastic jokes the entire time.

I can practically see Spencer pleading with me through the phone and I laugh. "Sure. I think I can do something like that. What time and where?"

"Awesome! I'm thinking about Tuesday. I'll call you when it gets closer and we'll figure out the rest of the details."

"Sounds good. Okay, I've got to do some homework and maybe sleep in there somewhere. I'll talk to you later."

"Good luck," Spencer says.

As I hang up the phone, I think about what Hillary said.

There's no way Spencer and I would make a good couple. He's like a golden retriever and I'm hot and cold about a lot of things. The only relationships I've had are fictional ones.

Besides, when Beau comes back to Boston, I'll never see the two of them as they continue building their business ventures. It's best to leave things alone and keep focused on school and the fantasy of a future with the guy I've been crushing on for the past four years.

2

SPENCER

I'm up early the next morning, trying to wake up on the third hole of the Hamilton Country Club. Golfing is a daily ritual for my father, and I go with him at least once a week. Maybe if I went as often as he does, I'd at least lower my score. As it is, I've already hit the ball into a sand trap and basically dug a sizable hole just trying to get it back on the green.

At least there's a golf cart. This is the first year my father has started using something besides his own legs to get around the course. He's not ancient, but I know his knees are bothering him lately. Getting them looked at by a doctor will probably happen when he's crawling around the green.

Since Dad won't talk much until we've made it through the eighteen holes, I have lots of time to think as we drive to the next spot.

The launch of the podcast I've been working on with my college roomie, Beau Olsen.

The last few tweaks of the audio platform we're setting up before we launch that.

All the marketing things we'll have to put into place before that.

Millie reminded me about that a couple of weeks ago. Getting an accountant to take over the books, as well as a few assistants for social media and any tech issues.

I smile as I think about her. I've only known her for about six months, but she feels like the sister I've never had. And ever since her brother went back to Bitter Springs to take care of some stuff, we've been hanging out a lot more.

"What are you grinning about?" my dad asks. I'm so surprised to hear his voice that I lose my balance and end up rolling out of the golf cart as he drives toward the next hole. He doesn't even realize I'm missing until he's about twenty yards ahead of me.

I jog over and slide into my seat, wishing I could go back thirty seconds and avoid this moment of shame.

"Everything okay, son?" he asks, turning to look at me with a laugh. He doesn't continue driving, which means we're getting behind on his race to end golf at the same time every day. For Richard Frederickson, it's a big deal.

"I'm great. Outstanding. This is fun, Dad."

"I think it's time you take me up on that golf instructor. He'll get rid of that slice in your swing after the first lesson." He drives forward, slower this time.

Plastering on a smile, I say, "Gee, thanks, Dad. I'm not trying to go pro here."

He shrugs. "You're usually so gung-ho to be on top of every-thing else you try. I figured I'd give you a push in the right direction if you're ready for it."

My phone rings and I see it's Beau. Maybe thinking about him enough summoned the universe to my side. Dad gets his clubs ready to tee off and I mouth that I'll be right there.

"Hey Beau, I'm glad you're still alive. It's about time you called me back."

There's loud music in the background and I'm worried he's in a bar this early in the day.

"We're celebrating." Beau chuckles and says, "I'm getting married. Put it on your calendar. Ten days from now."

It's like every coherent thought collides with the next one, and I end up with a mountain of jumbled thoughts.

"What do you mean you're getting married?" I ask. "You left here a few weeks ago without a girlfriend."

"Well, Cupid found me and now I'm engaged to the hottest girl around."

How many beautiful women could be in a place that's only a population of eight thousand? I bite my lip so I don't say that out loud.

"And her personality is great, right?" I say, hoping he's not just marrying her for looks. The fact that he's even talking about commitment has thrown me for a loop.

"Absolutely. She's the best."

"Have you known her for longer than eight weeks?" I know there are some places where people move from dating to engagement to marriage really quickly, but I never thought it would happen to Beau. He's been firmly in the no relationship category since I've known him. Maybe he's been put up to this. Or he's just kicked his drinking up a few notches.

"Trina Burkhead and I went to high school together. She was a few years younger, but we've been able to reminisce on the old days. My long bomb throw to win our homecoming game against our rivals."

That comment throws me for yet another loop. "You played football?"

Beau chuckles. "Yeah, man. I got injured after that game, so I'll never know how good I could've been."

I frown. "Dude, we were roommates in college and you never told me that. Are you sure you're Beau Olsen?"

"What are you talking about? Of course I'm Beau. Who else

would I be?" The slurring in his words alerts me to the fact that he's definitely been out all night. Colorado is two hours behind Massachusetts and it's only six-thirty in the morning here. Drunk Beau typically exaggerates the truth or even straight up lies. So him claiming to be engaged is some made-up story and I just need to ride it out.

"Spencer, I want you to be my best man. What do you think?"

"Uh, yeah, sure. Whatever you need, man." There's a long pause and it sounds like Beau is talking to someone away from the phone. "You're not really getting married, right?"

"Absolutely. It all works out."

"Are you coming back for the launch of the podcast?" I ask, hoping to get onto the topics I actually need answers to. Although, I'll probably have to call tomorrow to verify the responses when he's sober.

"I don't think so, bruh."

Now it's my turn to get frustrated. "You're bailing on it right when we need to get things going?"

"You'll be fine, Spencer. You're the host and the one who takes on all the responsibility anyway. Launch it how you want and I'll tell everyone about it."

Beau not caring about fame or money? Not that it's a guarantee in these endeavors, but I have to dream big.

He must be in love. Or he suffered a brain injury that affected his personality.

"And the voice actor platform?"

"Take care of that, too. Or I can do some stuff remotely." Beau's nonchalant voice is so different compared to the competitive spirit I heard in it weeks ago.

"What will you do out there?" I ask. He'd told me before that his family owns a car lot and a few other smaller businesses, but he'd always emphasized how much he disliked those occupations.

There's a moment of silence and then Beau says, "I've got a job lined up. Working for my fiancé's dad. I'll start at the bottom and work my way up."

"You, work in an office, wearing a suit day after day? Are you sure this is the Beau I met in college?" For him to say that he'd start at the bottom instead of finding every shortcut to make it to the top means something is wrong.

Beau chuckles and says, "I've already gone through the training and I actually like it. Talk to you soon, buddy." Yep, he's a goner.

The line goes dead and I stare at the phone for several more seconds, as if it will give me all the answers I'm searching for.

"Spence, let's go," my dad says, checking his watch. "What was that all about?"

"Business." I walk up and take a quick swing at the ball, not taking any extra time to line up the shot. It's the most non-Spencer thing I've ever done. But I suddenly want to get off this course and head back to the apartment, just so I can go over the game plan for the launches. The next time I get Beau on the phone, we'll be able to talk about the little details we need to sort out, fine-tuning the launches of our businesses. Because I can't see Beau making a one-eighty like that.

We get back into the golf cart and Dad drives forward at high speed to get to where our balls landed.

"Trouble with the new endeavors?" If it's one thing my father likes to talk about, it's business. He's been the king of the corporate world in his niche for as long as I can remember.

"Just a weird conversation with my business partner, Beau. He was drunk, but he said he's getting married and staying in Colorado."

"What's wrong with that? Marriage isn't the end of the world."

I frown. "Dad, he's never had a girlfriend or stuck with a job longer than six months. Now he's getting married *and* he wants an office job? That's the alcohol talking. The guy is practically allergic to work."

My dad is quiet for a few moments. We make it to the next hole but there's a group of guys getting ready to tee off, so we have a few minutes to chat. "Sometimes the big life stuff just clicks. Maybe this time it will be good for him. He might enjoy it."

"And if he hates it?" I ask.

Dad chuckles and says, "You sound like your mother when you moved out for college. Beau is an adult. He'll have to figure it out. But I thought you said he was drunk. Give him a day and you'll figure out what's really going on."

"True. It's just, there's a lot going on right now. It would be nice to have him here to iron out all the kinks in the launch process."

"This isn't like the Scotty situation."

I can hardly breathe at his words. Scotty Duncan is someone I'd been best friends with for years as we worked on the TV series *The Bright Years* together. One day we'd been working on the lines to a spinoff movie of the series and the next he'd disappeared without a trace. No one else was as worried about it and they eventually recast his part. But with him being a few years older, he was my mentor, and one of the best friends a guy could ask for in the film industry.

"All I needed was a note, a voicemail. A text, even to tell me why he left."

"I know, son, but people have reasons. It probably wasn't you. I'm sure he had his own demons to deal with and couldn't do it in the spotlight."

There had been rumors at the time that he'd had substance abuse problems, but I never saw that in him. Years later, I still feel betrayed by his lack of caring about me. Maybe that's why my knee-jerk reaction to Beau getting married and working for his father-in-law is to believe it's all a lie. Like his life is neatly tied with a bow, while I'm still trying to navigate adulthood.

My dad rests his hand on my shoulder. "Did you sign any paperwork for your businesses?"

I shake my head. We'd planned to get some paperwork started and signed, but I'd forgotten to finish filling out the requirements to get an LLC, so it's another item to add to my to-do list.

"Well, that might be a good place to start. Draw up some papers and have him sign them. It might help him decide if working with you is what he really wants to do with his life." He laughs, and then can't stop, slapping his knee.

"Really?"

My parents are some of the most encouraging people in the world. When I told them I was done acting after a few years of switching shows and trying to find a new fit for the older me, they didn't say another thing about it. They've always encouraged me to do what I wanted to, allowed me to fail or change at things and then guided me to the person I became. But they've always used a bit of humor to get the point across.

I don't think Beau and Millie have had the same experience.

"How's the sister doing? You should bring her around more often."

I'd brought Millie to one Sunday dinner with my parents a few weeks ago and now they always ask about her, even though my dad can't remember her name.

"I will."

"She seems like a good one. Quiet, but a nice girl."

With a chuckle, I say, "She was quiet because you and Mom kept talking through your questions so she didn't have a chance to say anything."

Dad shrugs and says, "We'll work on it. You might too. How come you bring none of your other girlfriends around?"

I frown, trying to figure out what he means by that. "Millie isn't a girlfriend. She's someone I've been hanging out with while her brother is gone."

"Well, she might be worth a second look."

Instead, I focus on hitting the ball and actually birdie it. It's been a long time since I've gotten the ball in the hole in anything less than four strokes.

"Now, if only your love life could be that easy," Dad quips.

"Ha ha, Dad. It's not that easy to find someone like Mom."

"You want someone just like Mom?"

Blowing out a breath, I say, "I know you had your issues, but you've been able to work things out and make a life together."

He nods, wiping a quick tear away as if I wouldn't be able to see it. "Life has been good, despite the obstacles."

"Wow, this is the most you've ever said when we're golfing. Maybe I need to see if you've got a fever." I step closer to him with my hand out, ready to feel his forehead. He steps back and shakes his head.

"I'm fine. You'll be fine. Just try to stick with one girl for longer than a week and see if you're compatible."

I don't want to talk about my love life with my father. So I nod and walk over to grab the ball out of the hole. I shake my head at the thought Beau would actually get married. I'll stick to what I've been doing all along: dating women and then moving on when things get serious. The way I took Scotty Duncan's departure, I don't think I'd survive the heartbreak of losing a woman I love.

3

MILLIE

I agreed to this. Well, technically, saying no to Evie while she's in her fairytale-like life with Owen is like telling a toddler they can't have a piece of candy they found on the ground. She's determined to find me a date for her wedding and I'm hoping I just make it to the big day. She went in through the Love, Austen app and set up a date for me within minutes of my giving her the go-ahead. And she said she'd give me fifty dollars, which I couldn't refuse. Poor college student, after all.

Dating isn't something I'm very good at. Growing up with five brothers and being the pseudo mom to most of them makes it hard for anyone to get past my defensive walls. My dad never had to say anything, because my brothers were so brutal. It doesn't make for the best memories in situations like this.

"Do you need anything else?" the server asks. I'm sitting at a diner trying to breathe deeply whenever the door opens. I've heard so many stories about people who think they're meeting one person online and end up meeting someone who didn't look remotely close to the profile picture. Maybe I should've done a video call or something beforehand.

Why am I trying to date when the guy I want to be in a relationship with is three thousand miles away?

Because I need the practice to get rid of the awkward side of me. It's what one of the gossip magazines I snuck from Hillary said. I'd never purchased one myself, but I've always been curious.

So I'm sitting at a diner alone and I've gone through two cups of water so far. I need to use the restroom, but what if he shows up fifteen minutes late and I'm not visible? I open the app and send him a message.

Me: I'm here at Cliff's Diner. How far out are you?

No immediate response comes through, so I dash to the bathroom. After I'm done, I wash my hands and hurry back to sit in my seat again.

Why am I trying to hurry? My insides are a mash of knots and I'm wondering if maybe this app could be the thing to help me start a relationship. Jordan is like a fairytale, a safe daydream that I can picture whenever I need to, while my real life is more like a movie where the girl has some major transformation, sans the happy ending.

There's no way I'd be lucky enough to find someone to spend forever with on the first try. I focus on the app now, scrolling back through the messages we exchanged over the past several days. They'd been fun and relaxed. What if he came, took one look at me and left?

Some people just aren't fans of red hair. But that's clearly in my profile picture.

I could be at home with my homework right now. I started school several months ago after quitting my nanny job. Since I'd been raising my siblings from the age of eleven, I'd always thought that being a nanny would be much easier than going to school. In reality, that's a lie.

It's a lot harder to parent someone else's kids, especially when everything I teach them is undone by the parents. I still love kids, but I need a nice long break, the chance to do my own thing.

Glancing down at my last comment to Sheldon Worthen, it says the message wasn't sent. I press the button to get it to send again.

"Hey Millie," a deep voice says. I look up to see Spencer. He takes a seat across from me before leaning over to look at the menu sitting on the table. He's humming a tune and I'm just trying to figure out why he's here.

I give a harsh whisper. "I'm supposed to be on a date. What are you doing here?"

Spencer looks around, surprised. "You're here for a date?" he asks. "Is this where you two were supposed to meet?"

"Kind of," I say, shrugging my shoulders.

"He didn't offer to take you somewhere nicer?" Spencer asked. The look on his face is pure bewilderment. I lean back and glance up as the door opens, but it's an older woman walking in. She waves to a friend sitting in a booth close to the front of the diner.

"Not everyone can afford what you pay for a date," I say, giving him a small smile.

One date a few months ago, he flew his current woman of that week to New York for the day to go to dinner and a Broadway show. Few people can compete with that.

"Maybe not for every date, but to make a good impression they should at least try. Or save their money to do so." He looks more serious than I've ever seen him. "How did you meet this guy?"

"On the Love, Austen app. How did you know I was here? Are you tracking me or something?" I scrunch my nose as I'm really kind of irritated. "I have several brothers who've been overly protective in the past, so I don't need you to sit and see the crash and burn of my dates."

"Millie, you're fine. But you can't keep thinking like that or that's how it will go. Manifestation and all that." He glances down at my phone and back up to my face, wrinkling his nose. "Do you trust that app?"

I nod. "Look at Rachelle and Landon, Dani and Miles, Kenzie and Trey, Evie and Owen. I mean, I feel like that speaks for itself, don't you?" Then I look at him a little closer and see he's dressed up in what I would deem going out clothes. "Why are you here?"

"I just figured I'd come in and hang out with you for a bit."

"Evie told you I was here, didn't she?" I shake my head when he responds with a nod.

"Yeah, she did. When I called you a bunch of times and you didn't answer, I got worried."

I go to my recent calls list and it's empty. "There's nothing from you.".

He lifts his phone to show me that he's called my phone number at least ten times. "I figured I'd keep trying to make sure I wasn't wrong."

"That's weird." I press his number to call it and am taken to the automated message saying my phone has been disconnected. "What day is it?"

"The fourteenth."

I groan. I was supposed to pay my cell phone bill by yesterday. A pit forms in my stomach whenever I make a mistake or forget things. So much for getting an A+ in adulting.

"Can I use your phone?"

Spencer hands it over to me and I type out a message to Evie. She'll be freaking out if she doesn't hear from me soon and I'd rather avoid a lecture later.

I search through his apps and am surprised to find the Love, Austen app. "What's this doing here?" I say with a smile, holding his phone up to show him the screen. He scowls and shakes his head.

"Miles downloaded it the last time we had a guy's night. I don't need it."

I roll my eyes at him. Of course, he's the one who has women lined up to date him. I don't think I've ever seen him with the same woman twice.

Out of curiosity, I see he hasn't even taken the test. I don't have time to worry about that right now, though. If my date attempted to contact me and I didn't get it, at least he'll get points for his effort.

I login. The message button is blank. He's now twenty minutes late. What kind of person ghosts someone they've just planned to meet?

I press the arrow back to the main screen and see a message that my top-three matches have recently been updated.

Did I ever check the originals? No. Should I check now? Probably not.

But does my body obey the brain? No. My thumb clicks on the notification and I see the profiles of three men pop up. In the third spot is a familiar picture, the one guy I was supposed to be meeting today.

I don't bother checking the other two guys, knowing I'd only feel like a failure for them not wanting to hang out with me.

"Are you all right?" Spencer asks. "Something wrong with your date?"

Shaking my head, I say, "No, it's nothing."

"How is school, by the way? What is it you're going into again?"

"It's going," I say, grinning. "I think I know what I want to be when I grow up."

Spencer leans forward, more engaged about some mundane bit of trivia about my life than I've ever seen anyone be, and he's smiling. "And what is that?" he asks.

"I'm going to be a business major with an emphasis in accounting."

Spencer pretends to snore and then laughs. "Why do you want to do that? I thought you were going to do graphic design."

"That was the original plan, but I found I don't like being told what to do in designing things. So I'll keep that for when I need a break from numbers."

"Your brother and I might need you to come work on our books once we get the company running. If he still wants to do it." He frowns and something passes over his expression. Before I can look deeper, it's gone.

I laugh, nodding. "Yeah, I don't see you and Beau keeping things in the black for long without someone to guide you."

Spencer laughs. "You know me so well."

"What are you doing here? Didn't you have a date with Veronica or Sarah or something?"

He sobers and says, "Natasha. And the date lasted all of three minutes. She broke up with me." He stares down at his hands as if they will keep him alive or something.

"Are you going to be okay?" I say, reaching over and putting my hand over the top of his. We've gotten closer ever since my older brother Beau came out to Boston to start a company with Spencer. We did a few things before Beau went back to Bitter Springs, Colorado, a couple months ago. When Spencer isn't dating his latest flavor of the week, we're usually hanging out.

"It's just weird to be dumped, you know. Usually it's me doing the dumping."

"Or ghosting," I add.

Spencer looks up at me with those hazel eyes that look a touch more blue today. "That was one time and I was horrible at getting the woman to leave me alone. I had to change my number."

"It's a good thing you never told her where you live. You

would've had to move," I say, taking a sip of the water in front of me.

Scrunching his nose at the thought, Spencer says, "Yeah, that's true. I love my apartment. I don't want to leave it."

"So what do you need to do then?" I ask, sounding a lot like my mother.

Spencer grins. "Maybe you can be my wing woman. You'll be the beast detector whenever I meet a new lady."

I laugh. "Beast detector. I think yours is broken or you weren't born with one."

"True," he says, playing with the paper from his straw. "I haven't been the best at picking normal women."

"You're so worried about the outside package you don't consider the inside one." My cheeks burn and I realize my filter around Spencer is slipping. I've always had opinions on a variety of topics, but I've learned through experience that keeping them to myself is the best course of action. Something about Spencer opens that gate wide though, meaning I say a lot more than I probably should to my brother's best friend.

He nods. "That's a very pointed remark. Explain."

I don't need to make things worse. "I didn't mean for it to sound like that."

Spencer gives me a half-smile, tipping his head down a bit and focusing all his attention on me. "I think you did. I'm not offended. The best kind of friend is one who can call out another one for their faults. So, Amelia Olsen, what can I do better when it comes to dating?"

"Honestly, I have no good experience in the dating realm. You're already way ahead of me there."

"Just tell me what you've seen." He's got his gaze locked on me and I'm pretty sure any woman might crack under the adorableness that this look is.

Wait, where did that come from? He's like my annoying older brother, right?

Taking in a breath, I say, "You date models, or women who could be models. Arm candy, if you will." I pause for a moment, waiting for his reaction. He only signals with his hand for me to continue.

"What are your normal conversations like?"

Spencer sits back and scans the restaurant before focusing on me again. "We talk about all sorts of things. The food, what the latest celebrity gossip is. The latest with their work or friend group."

I raise an eyebrow and say, "You're good with that?"

"What do you mean? Isn't that what normal relationships talk about?"

"Have you ever shared anything about your work, or what it was like to be a child actor?"

He swallows and shakes his head. "I usually avoid bringing that up."

"If you can't talk about those memories, or anything deeper than the surface-level 'getting-to-know you' stuff, is it even worth pursuing a relationship?"

He chews on his bottom lip and I suddenly want to slide out of the booth to go hug him. In a totally sisterly way, of course.

Wanting to change the subject quickly, I say, "Have you heard from Beau?" That's a safe topic.

"You haven't heard from him?" Spencer suddenly looks concerned.

I shake my head. "Not for at least a month."

Spencer frowned. "I talked to him this morning. He, uh, well–oh! Maybe he couldn't call you because of your phone being disconnected?"

"What's going on, Spencer?" I ask, trying to give him my sternest look.

"Well, first off, he was drunk."

I nod, knowing that whatever comes from Beau after he's had a few too many drinks is a wild card.

"He said he got a job back there and is getting married in ten days."

I laugh, shaking my head. "Yeah, that's a good one. You had my pulse racing for a few seconds there." I lean over to take a sip of water, my mind conjuring up an alternate universe where Beau gets married before the age of forty.

"I'm serious, Millie. He said he's marrying Trista or Tabitha Bankstock or someone like that."

Water gets trapped in my mouth and up to my nose, burning the insides as I try to blink past the sudden pain.

"Trina Burkhead?"

Spencer nods. "Yeah, that sounds right."

"He's definitely lying then. There's no way he would marry her."

"Why not?"

"Because she's the worst. He knows how much she tortured me in high school. Leave it to Beau to disappear without considering the wreckage he leaves behind." Another truth I've never admitted to anyone. I glance toward my cup. I don't taste any alcohol. Maybe truth serums are a real thing. Or maybe I'm just done with the crap.

"Well said, Millikins. He was supposed to be back long before we launched the podcast."

Spencer and Beau had been working on a weekly podcast talking about how they each got their start in the TV and film business. Granted, Spencer was on a popular television series for at least a decade growing up, while Beau has been on at least a hundred commercials for things like jock itch cream and other pills. He had a few appearances on a TV show as a server, but not enough to make him a household name.

"I don't know why you agreed to do it with him. My brother is a decent guy, but dependable, he is not."

"I kind of owe him, you know? He helped me through some of those first rough months in our freshman year of college.

After my parents temporarily split up, Beau helped me figure out a normal life outside of the studios, which I couldn't seem to do on my own."

Smiling, I feel a small measure of gratitude for my brother. Spencer is the most normal actor I've ever met. Then again, I don't think I've ever met another one face-to-face. I've only heard things here and there about child actors who go off the rails as they grow up.

"You've got the first few episodes recorded for the podcast, but weren't you working on another platform?" I ask.

Spencer grins. "Yes, we're about three months from launching that. It'll be a platform to help narrators and voice actors find work. I'm hoping to make it affordable to both the voice actors and those trying to contract them. The goal is to add a director's side as well, so those voice actors will be considered for movies and TV shows. Hopefully, it will all come together. I didn't realize there was that much to developing platforms like this."

"I can only imagine," I say. The time on Spencer's phone is later than I thought, and when I think of this failed date attempt, it makes me sad. "I need to get home. Pajamas are calling my name." I point to the jeans I'm wearing, and the blouse I borrowed from Evie has been scratching me just below my shoulder blade ever since I put it on.

"That sounds good to me. I mean, not your pajamas, but my own."

We both laugh and I reach into my side fanny pack to get my wallet. Before I can do anything, Spencer puts a twenty-dollar bill on the table and says, "Share an Uber?"

"You don't have to pay for that. I only got water."

"It helps the server for the time you waited. This night ended a lot better than it started for me. Why not pass it along? Let's go."

4

SPENCER

Time spent with Millie is time well spent. Even after breaking up with what she calls the "Flavor of the Week," it's like I can't even be sad for very long. She looks like a deer in the headlights every time she shares an opinion, and I wonder if my time with her is corrupting or helping her.

Our Uber arrives and I open the door, waving for Millie to get in. She bounces along the seat as she tries to scoot over, but there's some garbage on the floor of the car. Maybe she was trying to avoid that.

I give the driver Millie's address. Millie turns to me, confused. "Your place is closer. We'll just drop you off and I'll go after."

Shaking my head, I say, "It's fine. We'll head to your house and then I'll go home."

"That doesn't make sense. You'll be paying more."

I don't have words that can describe why I don't want her to just ride home alone. Sure, I'm still irritated that I was dumped, but what's worse than being dumped is being ghosted.

Millie taps at the window. "Oh, the phone store is still open. Can we stop there quickly? I'll run in and pay my bill."

She lifts her phone in the air and I'm reminded of sitting at the table and seeing a screen that looked like a stained glass piece of art put together by a six-year-old.

We walk into the store and I can't help but grin at the salesperson. She's not the happiest, probably because we just walked in ten minutes before closing. But since we're here, I've got a plan.

"I apologize," Millie says, walking over to the woman with a bright smile. "I just need to pay my bill to make it current. Hopefully that won't take too long." She opens her bag and pulls out a small wallet.

"Let's see," the woman says, asking for Millie's information. She gives it to her while I walk around the store, picking up a phone here and there.

The phone Millie owns has to be at least four years old. I can't imagine surviving with a phone that would lag that much. She needs a new phone, that much is clear, but how can I buy one for her without her knowing about it? Paying for an Uber is one thing, but a new phone? She'll fight me on it. Millie is like a pseudo-sister and, for some reason, I want to take care of her. Maybe it's her naïve character or just how much she's come to mean to me over the past few months.

The largest phone on display is the one I pick out first, but that would be my first choice. I put it back down and pick up a smaller one. Practicality-wise, it would fit in the small fanny-pack/purse she carries around.

Why am I even thinking about this for her? Because she's my best friend's sister and a good friend. I should take care of her while Beau is away. And the woman deserves a break on something. She's been saving everything she can ever since she quit nannying for a senator's family, and being a college student in this town isn't the cheapest.

"Okay, we've brought your account current. So give it an hour for the service to connect."

Millie nods and thanks the woman, folding up all the papers and tucks them into the small purse.

"Are you ready?" Millie asks, turning to look at me.

"Give me a minute. Maybe go tell the Uber driver I'll be right out."

She frowns but nods, disappearing through the door. It's when I turn to look at the woman behind the desk that I get the eye daggers of death.

I pull out a couple of large dollar bills and slide them over to her. "Take this as a tip for helping us out so close to the end of your shift."

The woman shakes her head. "I can't accept it. What can I help you with?" the woman asks, looking like she's hoping my request is easy.

"I need a new phone for my friend and an update to the billing for her account. Is there a way to just buy a phone and we can do all the transferring at home? That way you can get on with your night and she won't get cuts and slivers from the glass on the front of her phone."

"Is there a phone you're interested in?"

I walk over and point to the one I was looking at before. "This one. In white or pink, maybe?"

Janice, as her name tag says, nods and takes out some keys, walking into a back room lined with boxes. She comes out with one and says, "White is all we have left in this model."

"Perfect. Is there a way to pay ahead? Like her monthly billing, I mean." When the woman nods, I tell her to pay for the next year on Millie's account, and hand her my credit card.

With tears in her eyes, Janice taps away at her screen and says, "You have got to be the best boyfriend in the world."

I shake my head, trying to figure out why she would think

that. I mean, guy and girl together. Guy buys something expensive for a girl and that's assumed it's because of love.

"She's actually my best friend's sister. I'm just looking out for her."

The woman winks, as if I'm just lying about the whole situation.

"Well, if I were her, I'd lock you up with a key as soon as possible. I just broke up with my boyfriend because date nights were basically Netflix and chill for him."

I nod, giving her a strained smile as I walk out. I feel bad for Janice, but I tuck that away for another day. If I ever get past the first couple dates with a woman, I'll have to make sure I don't slip into the comfortable, easy zone.

I slide into the Uber and hand Millie the small bag with the phone inside. "This is for you."

She takes a moment to look inside and gasps. "What is this?"

I raise my eyebrows and say, "It's a cell phone. Some people can receive texts and phone calls without needing stitches from glass shards after."

I point to her phone and hold it up. "Please tell me you're done with this."

"It works just fine," she says, her eyebrows cinching together to make one line. She pushes the bag toward me. "This is yours."

Pushing back, I shake my head. "It's not mine because I bought it for you. It's white. There's no way I'm ever getting a white phone."

Millie looks like she's preparing for a duel. "Why did you do that? We're friends. Friends don't just purchase a brand-new phone that costs the amount of a month and a half of my rent just because."

"I'm sorry, Millie. But I couldn't let you suffer through using that relic any more. I try to take care of my friends."

"And do they always do the same for you?" she asks. I don't know why the question hits me so hard.

"Only the good ones."

"Let me pay for your Uber. Here's some cash," she says, going through her wallet. When she starts counting coins, I reach over and take the ten dollars in bills she's got.

"This is perfect." I open my door and hop around the car to open hers.

"Well, tonight didn't go as I expected, but thank you, Spencer. Thank you for this phone and for cheering me up tonight. I will pay you back."

I laugh and stick my hands into my pockets. "Oh, please. If anything, you helped me get out of a weird funk. See you soon."

I have the driver wait until she's inside before we pull away, my thoughts circling the words from the lady at the phone store.

When I'm having a hard time, finding someone to help has always been the right answer. Buying a new phone had never crossed my mind for any woman I've dated. Millie is like the little sister I never had. And if I want to spoil her now and then, I don't need to feel bad about it, right?

5

MILLIE

I stand against the closed front door for way longer than a grown woman should. The teen years weren't too far away, but I still feel like I should be past things like over analyzing situations this much.

How does this rate on the Jordan 3-Memory Scale? It's off the charts.

Jordan's actions were more just service oriented for an awkward teenage girl. Spencer has paid for so much when we've hung out. I try to total out everything I owe him just in the past month. Including the phone, at least fifteen hundred dollars.

Then there was that flash of attraction to him staring at me. I shouldn't let my mind wander into the unknown, but it's already conjuring up a scene where we date.

Am I shallow? I can't just start liking someone because he buys me gifts.

No, we're friends. Good friends, until Beau comes back and takes over.

Why would Spencer buy me a phone? Why would he crash my non-existent date?

He's always treated me like a little sister. Maybe that's what he would do if he had one.

"Everything go well on your date?" Evie asks, walking out of her room with her hair wrapped up in a towel.

How do I answer that? "Kind of. The guy never showed, but Spencer did."

Evie smiles. "Oh, that's right. I forgot I told him where you'd be. He sounded heartbroken on the phone, almost like a wounded puppy."

My stomach growls and I realize I never actually ate while at the diner. I put my purse and the bag from the phone on the counter and hunt for one of those big bowls of mac and cheese in the pantry. All I have to do is add water and microwave, which is perfect for this situation. And it's less than a dollar.

"Did you finally get a new phone?" Hillary asks, walking out from the laundry room. I don't think I've ever seen her do her laundry.

"Uh, yeah. Spencer kind of helped me out with it."

"Spencer?" Hillary and Evie say at the same time. They're standing next to each other and their body language is signaling that they are very, very interested in this conversation.

"Yeah, he showed up at the diner and my phone wouldn't work because I forgot to pay the bill, which I had money for, by the way. I just spaced transferring it and we ended up at the phone store. I paid for my bill and he bought a phone, which he gave me in the Uber."

Evie is grinning and near to tears. Hillary looks like she's trying to decide between the two truths and a lie game.

"That Spencer is a great guy," Evie says, winking.

Shaking my head, I say, "That he is."

"Was there a good-night kiss or anything?" Hillary asks, looking way more invested in this than our conversation the other day.

"No! We're just good friends. I mean, wouldn't that be weird to date my brother's best friend?"

"A quarter of the romance novels and movies in the world say no," Hillary says, letting out a deep laugh.

"Don't tell me that," I say. "There's no way Spencer could ever think of me in a romantic way. I've never been in an actual relationship. And he's dating girls like they come off the red carpet in droves. I'm good with keeping things the way they are. Simple and comfortable."

"Believe me, don't let things get complicated," Hillary says in an ominous tone. "You don't want to blur those lines and ruin the best thing you've got going."

I wave in front of her and say, "Are you talking to a theoretical someone? Or for me?"

Hillary shakes her head and says, "Both."

She strides out of the kitchen and disappears up the stairs. Evie sits at the table, her hands clasped together like she's a mom waiting at home after curfew for all the juicy details. Not something my own mother did, but I know a bunch of my friends had that relationship with their moms.

"We're just friends," I say right before Evie tries to add anything.

"That's great. I believe you. How's life?"

I chuckle and take the bowl out of the microwave, adding the dried cheese mixture and giving it a good stir. "Didn't we just have a life update yesterday?"

Evie laughs and says, "Probably. But I feel like I'm living through you since life has become sewing, nursing, and planning the wedding."

"Aren't those all things you love? You're marrying Owen, who's a good egg."

"Oh, of course. I just need a dose of Millie more often than not."

I drag my bags over to the table, knowing I'll need to set up my new phone at some point. I should probably buy a phone protector and case this time. If I drop it and everything cracks, I'll never be able to face Spencer again.

As I eat the mac and cheese, Evie takes the phone out of the case and oohs and aahs over it. She then sets to work, turning it on and fiddling with the buttons.

"Do you mind if I get it working for you?"

I blink a few times, wondering if I've landed on some strange alternate house universe. "You want to set it up?"

"Yeah, I enjoy getting it all changed over."

"Good, because I've never done it myself. I usually have them do it at the store. Then again, the last phone I got was before I moved to Boston and it's seen some things." We both laugh.

I eat while she works through the details with the operator. Who knew you could call someone this late at night and get help? There is help at all hours apparently. Another life lesson to add to my brain.

My mind swings back to Spencer, the grin he gave me when he handed me the bag in the car. Why is he still single? From my angle, he's a catch, with his kindness and his humor. He's always up for an adventure and is a hard worker, although he tries to hide that sometimes.

And then, just a few short minutes later, Evie hands me the phone as if it's the most fragile thing in the world. Which in my case, I should probably treat it as such.

"Thank you," I say, pulling it over and checking out the screen. There are a few apps that didn't transfer over, but at least the hardest part is done.

A few seconds later, my phone dings in a different tone than I'm used to. There's a number twelve over the phone app and then twenty-five text messages for the text app.

"Who in the world is trying to contact me?" This is more contact I've gotten in one day in my life. I usually don't get to this level in a week, unless Evie or my other roommates get going in the group text.

I turn the voice message on speaker and wait as it gets to the actual message.

"Mills, I have something I wanted to share with you. Call me back. Beau."

At least I know he's alive. The guy left two months ago and not that we've always been super chatty to one another, but it's been radio silence on his end for weeks.

I delete that one and the next one starts playing.

"Millie, seriously? Are you screening my calls? Call. Me. Beau."

"Does he always talk to you like that?" Evie asks, frowning at the phone, as if it would relay her thoughts to my brother.

"Pretty much."

Voicemail number three comes up, but this time it's my mother's voice.

"Amelia Jane Olsen. Why haven't you called your brother back? It's an important announcement, and he really needs your support."

Using my full name is never a good thing, but then again, my parents used it often when I lived at home.

"Amelia, your mom is pestering me to get you to answer your brother's phone call back. Call him." My dad sounds as bored as always in his voicemail.

And then my phone rings, Beau's name popping up. "That's good timing," I mumble.

Evie waves and walks back into her room when I answer the call.

"Hey," I say.

"Hey is all you have to say? It's been hours, Millie. Almost an entire day since I called you."

I frown. No one in my family is ever this excited to tell me anything. "Did someone die?"

Beau laughs and says, "No, well, you could say that my bachelorhood is about to."

"You're engaged? It's not a joke?" I ask, trying to figure out who he could've dated and proposed to that quickly. Nine weeks in Bitter Springs is a lot longer than here in Boston, especially since there isn't much to do. I don't want to think about the last part of the conversation Spencer had mentioned earlier, the name of the person my brother would hypothetically be marrying.

"Would I be this persistent if it were a joke? The wedding is in ten days, so we can go on our honeymoon before we head out on the road together."

"Why would you be traveling on the road?"

"I'll be working as a scout for the Idaho Grizzlies baseball team. Trina's dad is having me start at the bottom of their company so I can learn everything before moving up."

It takes some work, but I try to picture my brother scouting anything. Sure, he played a little baseball growing up, but I doubt he has the skills to spot talent for a Triple A baseball club.

Hesitating another moment, I finally ask, "Who are you marrying, Beau?"

"Trina Burkhead." I can tell from the sound of his voice that he's grinning from ear to ear.

"You're serious?" My lungs constrict. Four years of high school with Trina was bad enough, but to have to endure every family gathering from here on out with her? I don't know if I have the constitution for it.

Another laugh before he says, "Yeah, Millie. I proposed a couple of days ago, but since you have such a hard time picking up the phone, you're just hearing about it now."

"Why so fast? Did you get her pregnant?" Apparently, my filter broke.

There's no laughter on the line now and I'm wondering if I

hit a nerve. "No, and don't you say that again," Beau says, his voice edged with a serious tone.

"You could always do the long-distance thing. Wait until the end of whatever job you have going on and then get married." If he started dating her the day he flew home two months ago, that still seems fast to go from dating to engaged to married.

"Come on, Millie. I don't expect you to understand something like this. You've never even had a boyfriend."

That cuts deeper than it should.

Beau's voice is softer this time, as if he's trying to apologize for his harsh words without really apologizing. "We met at a community thing and then we've been together just about every day since. I know I said I'd probably never settle down, but this is different. I want to spend my life with her."

And I can't really argue with that.

"You know what she did to me, right?" I say, using one last attempt to sway him to my side.

"I know, but she's not like that, sis. Not anymore. We've talked about it and I know she'll want to apologize in person. We'll be starting the festivities on Monday, so hurry and catch a flight home."

"I don't fly, remember?" I say through gritted teeth.

"You used to. It's not that hard to board a plane and land in a place far away within a couple of hours, Millie. You should try it again."

Panic floods me at the thought of boarding a plane. The last time we flew, it was through an awful rainstorm. Turbulence with the up and down of the plane and then the plane almost got hit by lightning. Once we landed, I knew there was no way I could chance flying again. "I'm good. And now's not a great time. I've got a couple of finals to study for and a paper to write."

"Aren't you going to one of those online schools where you can pack in as many credits as you want? That means you should be able to do it whenever and not when a professor demands you do it. Come home, Millie. Mom is beside herself that she wants the whole family here for the wedding."

His comments sting, but I pull up the defense wall that I've built from growing up in my family.

"The semester is over at the end of the month and if I head out to you, I won't have time to finish everything. Also, I don't have a vehicle to drive home and I don't have the funds to rent one."

"Mom says we'll work out the details. She just wants you to come home."

Home. I consider this more of a home than Bitter Springs ever was. There are too many things that make it hard to go back when nothing has changed there.

"Just Photoshop me into the pictures." And for the first time in my life, I hang up on someone.

Maybe it's because I'm not strong enough to debate with him right now. But for him to marry my arch nemesis from high school? I can't even fathom standing in the same room with her and watching her join the Olsen family.

Why would she go for Beau, anyway? He doesn't have a trust fund to comfortably carry him through life, even if he acts like he does. She's never been one for knockoff brands.

I turn off the phone and head upstairs. After the night I've had, I need to just mindlessly watch TV and pretend my life doesn't exist for a while.

6

MILLIE

It hasn't even been ten minutes since I wake up the next morning and turn on my phone when it rings. My mom's name is scrolling across the screen and I know what it's going to be about. That snitch of a brother.

I knew I'd have to face the music at some point. Despite the dozens of texts and voicemails, I just deleted them all and went back to studying for my test.

"Hi Mom," I say, keeping my voice low.

"Amelia Jane, you had better be coming to the wedding. This is the first one in our family and we need to be supportive. Especially with the Burkheads there. They're already hogging most of the room for the rehearsal dinner."

I try to keep my emotions in check as I picture that scene. There are only a handful of places close to my parents' house that would work for a wedding. And since we're related to most of the people in Bitter Springs, having the Burkheads over-shadow our family in number would be a novel experience.

"You know what she did to me, Mom. I'm not coming."

Spencer's grinning face appears over the railing of the stairs, and he walks over and sits by me.

"What are you doing?" I mouth.

"I was bored," he whispers.

"You've grown up since then," my mother says, pulling me back to this conversation, "and so has she. I want the whole family to be there for this."

Spencer is staring at me, as if he can hear everything she's saying. With the volume of her regular voice, I wouldn't be surprised if he can.

"What's going on?" he asks.

"My mom is calling about the wedding," I whisper.

He leans over and tugs the phone from my hand. "Mrs. Olsen, this is Spencer. How's it going?"

From that distance, her voice sounds like the Charlie Brown mom. Spencer nods and then says, "She needs to make up her own mind about it. You can't force her."

Another minute or two of talking and I scoot closer, so my body is right flush with Spencer's on the couch. He smells insanely good today. Not that I've noticed his particular smells before, but something about his cologne hits me differently.

I lean my ear up to hear what they're talking about, trying to push away some of those thoughts. This is my brother's best friend. I can't ruin that.

"... She needs to be here. What would the town think if she didn't come home for a celebration like this?"

Spencer shakes his head. "I don't think the town should worry about it."

"Spencer, will you try to talk her into coming? Maybe you can be her date or something. Jordan Dietrich is one of the groomsmen and he's coming with a plus one. She'll be heart-broken if she comes by herself."

Nothing like my mother never ever forgetting the one crush I had on the only cute guy in Bitter Springs from middle school to when I moved to Boston. This is why I don't tell her things.

"I'd be happy to be her date. But I'm not pushing her to go to something she doesn't want to attend."

Would he be okay as my date? I should not be locking onto that detail. Too late, it's already on a loop in my brain.

I can hear my mother's sobs and I close my eyes, knowing the drama has only begun. That was a big reason I moved to Boston. To do my own thing on my timetable.

A gruff voice gets on the call. "Millie?"

"This is Spencer, sir. Let me give her the phone."

Spencer hands it to me, giving me a tight smile. My dad has always been a straight shooter and I'm not quite prepared for a debate with him today.

I clear my throat, not sure what to say that won't betray the hurt of this whole situation.

"Amelia Jane, we're going to need you here for this wedding."

I gulp and say, "Dad, I've got school and I'm trying to find another job so I can pay rent. I can't just up and head back without more time."

There's a long moment of silence and I wonder if we've been cut off. Then I can hear the heavy breathing.

"I'll pay your rent for the next six months."

Did I just hear him correctly? The man who had us paying for our own clothing since we were old enough to earn money is going to pay my rent?

"You don't even know how much it costs. That would hurt the family," I say, doing my best to be considerate of the other siblings still at home.

"How do you know anything about our finances? We've got plenty to share. Just come home."

"I don't have the money to rent a car to get there, Dad."

"You can't just suck it up this one time and take a flight?"

Before I say something I'll regret, I shake my head. "No. That's non-negotiable."

"I've been looking at a few vehicles that way for the lot. I'll find something you can drive here. But you'll need to be here by the weekend. There's a lot going on and already planned events for it."

I shouldn't be even contemplating going, especially with who I'll have to confront when I get there, let alone nightmares I'd revisit. Maybe it's the fact that I want to see my dad follow through on something he offered. Or morbid curiosity at how this whole thing is going to go.

"Why is it such a big deal? You can always send me a link to watch it, right?"

"Don't embarrass us like this, Amelia. You've got to be an example to your brothers."

I have five brothers–Beau, Carl, Danny, Eric, and Frank. I don't think I've seen them in anything nicer than the simple khakis and button-up shirt my mom makes them wear to church on Sundays. There's still always dirt smudged somewhere when they're around.

I don't want to agree too quickly and I'm almost tempted to ask him to write down everything he's offered me, just in case he decides to go back on his word.

Six months of free rent and I won't have to pay for a vehicle to drive out to Bitter Springs. It would be good to see my younger brothers. Every time I see them, it's like they've grown another foot.

"Okay, rent for six months, as well as a vehicle to drive there and another to drive back, along with gas." I'm pushing my luck, but I might as well negotiate everything I can for the discomfort I'll go through for this wedding. "I'm going to send you a text about these conditions. If you agree with them, text me back yes."

There are several more moments of silence and then he says, "Fine."

The call goes silent and I immediately open my messaging

app to text him that information. It's the closest I have to actual paperwork to prove that's what he said.

Spencer is staring at me with wide eyes. "You have a very complicated relationship with your family."

I don't know if it's because, from the outside, we look more like hostage negotiators than a family, but it's true. "Yes. I learned when I came out here that I need everything in writing."

"I had no idea. Beau never mentioned anything like that before."

I give Spencer a side-eye and say, "Beau is cut from the same cloth, except he's learned to be more subtle about his cutthroat ways. In a weird twist of fate, though, I still love him and my family. It's just hard to be around them for lengthy periods of time because I can never break out of the old role I grew up with. The eldest daughter with a people-pleasing tendency and a need to be no trouble."

Spencer blinks twice and says, "Wow, that's a lot. I guess I don't really know what that's like. Being an only child has a few benefits."

"If I got a dollar every time I wished I was an only child growing up, I'd probably be a multi-millionaire."

"So you're going?" Spencer asks.

Is it awful that Spencer bought me a phone and now my dad is going to pay my rent? I've worked hard the past few years to be independent, to stick out the tough things so I didn't have to go crawling home as a failure. And I've done it. The hardest part is accepting help after so long in survival mode.

"Would you actually be my date?" Why does my voice have a wobble to it?

Spencer grins. "Absolutely."

I click my phone on to check the message and see "Yes" pop up as a response from my dad. "I don't really have a choice now. It's hard to turn down free rent."

And if I have to go through a real-life nightmare, I can't help but think Spencer is the one I want to be next to me.

7

SPENCER

Hanging out with Millie always leaves me energized. I don't know why, but I enjoy trying to pull back the layers that make her tick. And now that we've known each other for over six months, it's like she's finally warming up to me, getting used to me as a haven for her opinions. It helps when her brother isn't around, though. That's when she shuts up like a clam.

I called her this morning, wondering how she likes the new phone. It went straight to voicemail, which is why I swung by her house. I don't have much on the schedule today and I'm hoping she'll go to one of the old-time movies with me.

Thinking of Beau, I'm still shocked he's really getting married. What will that do to our business? Will he move his wife out to Boston so we can continue? I can't see him as a professional baseball scout and we've still got a lot to do for the launch of the podcast. We want to be making waves with it at the beginning to get as many listeners as possible. I don't know how long the scout thing would really pan out anyway.

Sure, the content of our podcast show is appealing, mostly because there are a lot of people in the world who imagine what it would be like to be an actor. I'm here to tell them that it's not all glitz and glam. There are long, long days of filming, and then promoting things on late night shows and radio shows make it harder. Then again, winning an award does help fuel the desire to keep going.

Beau asked me a few months ago why I don't get back into the on-screen stuff. I didn't have a good reason then, but once we started these two ventures, it gave me a chance to put it all into words. I like the freedom my career gives me now.

I can do all my voice acting from home, well, almost all of it. There are a few projects that need me in a studio to complete, but most days, I make my schedule. There's no pushing through a sore throat to finish the day of filming, and I've done it long enough to know how long things will take me.

After being a child actor, having the paparazzi follow me around while I was on *The Bright Years*, this is pure heaven. It also helps that I've grown up and don't look a lot like my character back then. Sure, that career helped set me up for the life I live now, but I don't need to keep seeking fame and trying to get a star on some sidewalk. Mental and emotional health is just as important as staying in shape physically.

"What brings you here?" Millie asks, turning off her phone after the discussion with her parents.

"I was curious how the new phone was and if you wanted to go see a movie or something today. But now I'm wondering if you're in the right profession. You might need to get a job as a lawyer or something with those debate skills."

She chuckles. "I promise that is a once in a lifetime kind of deal. My parents have never offered me anything they didn't think I could work for."

I nod, understanding a lot more about the Olsen dynamic now. Beau and Millie might've grown up in the same household, but this is the first time I've seen Millie stand up for herself.

I nod. "I get that. Are you all right?"

A tear slides down her cheek and she tries to wipe it away too fast, poking herself in the eye. I'm not sure how to react until her shoulders shake. Is she laughing?

"I'm alive. Does that count?" She sits up with a sigh, scooting away from me and pulling her legs up to her chest, hugging them tightly.

"Yeah, that's a start, at least."

Millie's body shudders, and I hear a slight cry. I'm not sure when the laughter turned to tears, but I guess I've just got to ride out this rollercoaster. "It's just that of all the women he could marry, why pick her? And I'll have to relive my humiliation for the rest of my life."

"What did she do that was so bad?" I ask, smoothing down her hair.

"She stole my clothes from the locker room and soaked them in the showers. I had to wear my P.E. clothes for the rest of the day, and they weren't the most flattering thing. She also covered me in lunch from my tray and an entire list of other things."

I pause a moment and then say, "You don't think she's grown up since then?"

Millie leans back, giving me a look that makes me smile. She's so disgusted. "Do mean girls ever turn nice?"

With a shrug, I say, "I'm not really sure about that one. I thought you were homeschooled."

"Yes, until high school. My mom wanted to make sure that we had a high school experience."

"So, when are you heading out?" I ask. "To the wedding, I mean."

"I'm just waiting for my dad. I don't want to rent a car."

"What about a flight?" I ask.

She cringes. "I just had a terrible experience the last time I flew. So it's better for me to drive."

"How long of a drive is that?"

"Probably two and a half days. I usually stop and sleep somewhere at night."

I study her face and am surprised how determined she is to do that when a flight would take about four hours, not sixty. I'd heard a lot about her driving skills from the other roommates and wondered if she'd make it safely to Bitter Springs.

"Do you have problems falling asleep when you drive?"

"With enough caffeine, I do pretty well."

Blowing out a breath, I say, "Do you want me to drive with you?" Why I offer to suffer through the torture of a long drive is beyond me, but I don't want her to get hurt.

Her eyes widen and she says, "I would love that if you're up to it."

"I've never really done a road trip like that. So I guess it would be an adventure."

"You've never been on a road trip? How did you do family vacations? All I can remember is the stinky smell of socks in our large van and one of my brothers throwing up all over."

Cringing, I say, "Um, yeah, I didn't live through trauma like that. And you still want to drive?"

"Well, I'm an adult now, so it's different when I can decide if I need to stop for a bathroom break or to get something to eat."

"Wait, you didn't stop for bathroom breaks?" This is turning into more of a horror story than I originally thought.

Millie lets out a long breath and says, "We just had to hold it until Dad would stop for gas. I learned to ration my water intake on those trips."

"And that was normal for you?" I ask.

She shrugs. "That's all I ever knew."

"My family didn't take long trips, but we always stopped if someone had to pee."

Millie laughs. "It's a privilege you probably didn't even realize back then."

"What about this Josiah Denton?"

"Jordan Dietrich," Millie says, her mood sobering. "He was a guy I liked in high school."

"And did anything happen?"

She waves her hand in the air and says, "We had a couple of fun hangouts before I came out here to be a nanny."

"Have you talked to him since?" I now have so many questions. Like, is a hangout slang for something other than sitting on opposite ends of a couch to watch a movie or play a game? The way she makes it sound, these were significant moments for her.

Blowing out a breath, she shakes her head. "No, it was never the right time."

I hold my question for a few moments before I have to let it out. "What are you waiting for? If you still like the guy, this could be your chance to make something happen."

Millie looks conflicted, her lips pursed like she isn't sure what to think of my words. "I always thought I'd have been on a few more trips and have something to show for my time here."

That reveals a lot. I'm guessing she's got a big crush on a nice guy.

"Sounds like this Justin guy will be there. Anything you want me to do to get his attention?" I blurt out. The way she looks like a wounded puppy makes me want to protect her.

Millie's eyebrows raise, and she points to herself. "Are you sure you want to be my date? What happens if you date some woman tomorrow? She'll probably want to go with you."

"No, I'm not hard launching any relationship by taking a woman to a wedding right now. It'll be good for both of us. We can make Jonathan realize how amazing you are and I'll be there whenever you have to square off with Trista and I'll have someone on my arm so I don't have every grandma in the place trying to set me up."

Millie laughs again. "It sounds like you're used to that."

"Sadly, it's a curse."

"Well, I'll gladly be your grandma-protector. I have a few cousins who aren't married and there would definitely be some matching going on if you were there alone."

I frown, trying to understand the dynamics of their family. "So, they wouldn't try to set anyone up with you?"

Her smile disappears and she shakes her head. "No, if I get married, then they'll lose their dependable babysitter."

"They won't make you do that while you're there for the wedding, right?"

She sighs and says, "If they don't, I'll wonder if I'm in the right family."

The more I get to know Millie, the more amazing she is. Selfless, kind, and a stubborn streak that I've only seen a few times.

There's that protective streak popping up again. At least I can help her through whatever happens in the next week.

8

MILLIE

It sinks in an hour later with my hand stuck in a bucket of popcorn at a black-and-white movie with Spencer. How am I going to face all those people who think I've made it in life because I live in Boston? For the amount of work it was to nanny, the pay was below minimum wage, despite the perk of having a car to run the kids around with. I do miss that.

I absolutely love Boston, but for all different reasons than I came here for. I love the ability to get to so many places using public transportation. And there is so much history around every corner.

The problem is that my family doesn't understand that. Money is the end all and the biggest indicator of success. I don't see it that way, though. For the little I'd learned before moving away, I feel like I've been successful just getting to this point in my life, being able to act on my own ideas and opinions without being shamed to conform.

The movie ends and I wait for Spencer just outside the restroom. I get a text from my dad with a link to a large truck. This is a joke, right? I click the link and find that it's a six-door truck.

Yep, an extra two doors in one truck. I think my dad had sold one a long time ago, but I've never seen something like that. How am I supposed to park that thing? My brain spins as I try to think through the logistics of this. And then I text him back.

Me: You found a nice compact car, right?

Dad: No, the truck is the one I need. It shouldn't be too far away from you.

I glance back at the link and see that it's nearly an hour away. The old Millie would have jumped through every hoop to make this arrangement work, but I'm not that girl anymore.

Me: Dad, I can't even get to their house because there's no public transportation there.

Dad: Why are you being so difficult?

I type out several answers, feeling bold that I'm not doing this face-to-face, but I eventually delete all of them.

Me: I'm not being difficult. I'm just telling you that the guy needs to deliver the truck to me or find something else that I can drive cross-country.

Spencer comes out of the bathroom and says, "What's up? You look like you're gearing up for a hostile takeover."

I shake my head and sigh. "My dad found a vehicle to drive to my hometown."

He looks suspicious and says, "And that's bad, why?"

"It's kind of hard to explain." I don't even know where to begin, but then again, I don't need to burden Spencer with this kind of stuff.

Another text comes through.

Dad: The guy said he'll deliver it this afternoon. Make sure you're packed and ready to go. We need you here tomorrow.

I laugh out loud and shake my head. I'm glad that I stuck to my guns.

Me: I'll be lucky to be there in three days if I leave tonight. I'm not driving in the dark, Dad.

Instead of getting a text from my father, it's from my mother's number.

Mom: Be careful, dear. Drive safely and take as many breaks as you need to. The activities don't start for a few days. Hurry home to us.

I really want to ask them why they're pushing so hard for this. And why they're making it seem like I'm the Prodigal Daughter. The only thing they've used me for is caretaking. It's not like I'm the jewel of the town and everyone will miss me if I'm gone. I just wish they weren't pushing to look good for everyone.

I create a text message for both parents.

Me: I'll be fine. I'll bring gas receipts for reimbursement. See you soon.

And that's when I need to see if Spencer is really up for this. He had to run into a shop close to the theater and once he comes out, I hold up my phone with a picture of the monstrosity.

"What's that? Are you taking me to a monster truck rally?" he asks, looking like a kid on Christmas morning.

"Have you never been to one of those?" I ask.

He shakes his head.

"Well, what if I were to tell you that this is our ride to Colorado?"

"I would think you were crazy. That isn't a Photoshop job?"

"No, this will be delivered to the house this afternoon. Are you still up for a road trip?"

"Sure. I mean, I need to go to the store and get a few things, but I should be good if we leave this weekend."

I cringe and say, "Well, what if we get a start this afternoon?"

"You're joking, right?"

That's when I laugh. "You look like you're terrified of something. We're not running a marathon, just sitting in a truck for hours on end."

Spencer studies my face and, for some reason, the attention makes my insides flip flop. This is Spencer, Beau and Jack's best friend. There's no way a relationship beyond friends would happen between us. But the guy has paid me more attention than any man in my past, aside from those couple of times with Jordan. Is that why I'm catching feelings?

No. Not going to happen. He's my date for the wedding and that's it. We're going as friends. Buddy, buddy friends.

"You're serious, aren't you?"

"Absolutely. The sooner we get out of here, the sooner we'll be at the point of no return."

He shakes his head. "I still don't get why you're doing this."

"It's complicated, Spencer. It's just the Olsen way of life."

"Well, I guess we'll have plenty of time to talk about it on the drive."

I frown. "What do you mean?"

"It's like thirty-something hours to your hometown, right? What did you think we'd do?"

"The only road trips we've ever taken meant we had to be absolutely quiet or there were punishments."

"Punishments? For kids? I'm not sure how you were quiet. My family does a lot of talking during trips like that."

I raise an eyebrow. "So you've driven across the country before?"

"Er, no. But it will be an adventure. I'll go get packed so we can head out. Is there anything you need me to pick up at the store?"

"Red Vines, Gummy Bears, and Kettle cooked chips."

"Okay, sounds like a recipe for a canker sore, but whatever."

He waves and walks back to the vehicle parked in the drive-way. I've never really paid attention to Spencer's lifestyle, but his car is nice. Sleek and clean, with the license plate firmly attached on all sides. Definitely not something we're used to driving back home.

It's then I realize I haven't even done laundry. At least Rachelle, our landlord, put in a larger washer a month ago when the other one died. Maybe I can get enough done that I won't have to do it at home.

Home. It's such a strange thing, because Boston feels a lot more like home than Bitter Springs ever did.

As I pack the non-clothing items, I try to think of how long I'll be there. Three days to drive, a few days for whatever wedding activities they have planned, and then another three to get back. In the middle of that, I'll have to work on my homework so I'm not scrambling to finish before the deadlines.

Can I make it through all of that and deal with the past trauma while seeing my high school bully become part of our family? I'm strong, but I don't know if I'm that strong.

9

SPENCER

"I'm heading out this afternoon, Mom," I say through the phone. I'm walking down the snack aisle at the closest grocery store to my apartment.

"You're going to survive that drive?" Mom says with a chuckle. "Don't forget the Dramamine."

I shake my head. "It's not that bad. We're just driving across the country, not doing loops on a ride at Disney."

"Are you doing all right?" she asks, her tone softening.

"I'm great. Why?"

"Your father was telling me you two had a good chat during golf. I know your friend getting married will disrupt your life in a way, and I wanted to make sure you're okay."

I love my parents, but sometimes they go a little overkill on things like this. One downside to being an only child.

"I'll be fine, Mom. He's getting married and taking a job as a baseball scout. I don't want to hold him back if that's what he really wants to do."

"This isn't the same as Scotty—"

"I've got to go, Mom. I'm supposed to be at Millie's place in about forty-five minutes, and I still have to pack."

There's a long pause on the other end. "Just remember that we love you. Call if you need anything while you're gone."

"Will do." I say goodbye and hang up. I'm not sure why both parents keep trying to bring up Scotty Duncan and his departure lately. Maybe they're just trying to help me, but it feels a lot more like a stab to the heart every time they mention my old costar.

Are there a lot of similarities between Beau and Scotty? Sure. But at least Beau is giving me a few days warning that what I'd envisioned for my life ever since we started these endeavors is going to be different. A solo journey instead of with someone else.

I pick up the snacks Millie requested and buy some jerky, nuts, and some fruit for me. Old habits die hard when it comes to health.

The media had highlighted the fact that I'd had a chubby stint before a growth spurt and it's always stayed with me. Scotty was the one who got me through that. Helping me figure out better options to eat and how to lift weights.

Man, I still miss that guy.

The benefit is I still have Jack. And Millie.

I can't focus on people leaving me behind. I've got to find a way to move forward at my own pace and not worry about the overall results. Maybe I'm meant to take another path, and I just have to accept that.

The thought is kind of depressing.

Let's get through the wedding and then I can reevaluate from there.

10

MILLIE

Three hours after getting home from the movies, I've done the bulk of my laundry and packed up all my school stuff. I don't have many options in my closet for dresses to wear to a wedding, but I'll have to make do. I don't need to spend all my savings on a couple of pieces of clothing that I'll rarely wear again.

Evie has always said I can borrow anything in her closet, so I pack two options from there and hope for the best.

Then I think about Trina with her mischievous grin and blow out a breath. I can handle this event because I'm getting my rent paid. After that, I'll avoid any future event she attends.

Hillary knocks on my door. "Hey, there's some guy outside with a monster truck. It's like a limo. Are you buying that thing?"

I walk over to the window where I can see outside. It's a long bed Ford truck, with six doors, just like the picture my dad sent.

"I'm not, but apparently my father did."

Hillary glances around at the bags on my bed. "Are you going somewhere?"

With a sigh, I say, "Beau is getting married to my high school nemesis."

"For real? So you're going home. Are you taking the revenge approach? I've got some ideas if you need them."

I'm too stunned to say anything at first and then I burst out laughing. "I'm going to figure out the situation when I get there. But if I need ideas, I'll text you."

"Perfect." She turns to leave, and I notice she's wearing an Elsa costume.

"Wow, you've had a lot of princess parties lately."

Hillary stops and turns to look at me. "That's the truth. I'm used to the holiday season being big, or summer, even. But this spring has been a lot of events and birthday parties. Whatever helps me pay the bills, I guess."

I laugh and shake my head as she walks away. Heading down the stairs quickly, I meet the man at the door.

"Delivery for Amelia Olsen?" he asks. I'm surprised my parents didn't add in my middle name as another way to tell me they're disappointed that I didn't leap at the opportunity to drive across the country for my brother's sudden nuptials.

"That's me," I say. "Do you need me to sign anything?"

"As long as you have a check to deliver, that should be good."

I glimpse the large number on the paper in his hand. "Are you talking about a check to pay that amount?" I point to it and he glances down before nodding.

"Yes. That's what it's being sold for."

I try to smile, even though I want to hurl that my father would pull this. I don't have a fraction of this in my bank account, despite my attempts at keeping things simple.

"Let me make a phone call really quick," I say, pulling out my phone as I turn toward the kitchen.

My dad picks up on the fifth ring, which is good because I

don't know if I can handle the pressure of the guy staring at me, wanting his money for the monster truck outside.

"Hey Amelia, have you left yet?"

"No. Funny story, actually not really funny, but the guy is here to deliver the truck and says he's waiting for a check. It would take me at least ten years to earn the money for it, so I don't know why you want me to pay."

"Whoa, whoa, slow down. I wouldn't make you pay for it. Hand the phone to the guy and let me talk to him."

This is so different from any other interaction I've had with my father that I take at least ten seconds to register his words. I walk over and hand the phone to the delivery guy. "My dad is the one you'll want to talk to."

The guy rolls his eyes and gives me a look like I'm just some spoiled kid, instead of the reality that is my life. He listens for several moments before nodding and saying, "Sounds good. I'll check that and then give her the keys if all goes through."

He pulls the phone away from his ear and hands it back to me.

"What do I need to do?" I ask my dad, not wanting to stand there awkwardly anymore.

"Just give it a minute. He should get a notification that I wired the money to his account and then you'll be ready. See you soon, cupcake."

I wrinkle my nose. What has gotten into my family? I've never heard my father call me anything other than my name. Has Trina captured them all for some weird science experiment gone wrong? Life was normal until she came into the picture.

"Looks like the transfer is complete. Here are the keys. Reminder that it's diesel, so the green handled–"

"I know what diesel means," I say, gritting my teeth. Nothing like mansplaining something I've known since birth.

He opens the door to the driver's side and I glance in. "Any questions about the rest of it?"

I step up into the cab, checking all the usual features for this model. My dad has been a car dealer in our small town for at least fifteen years. I've driven several types and brands of trucks, but never one this long. If I can make it out of the city with my nerves intact, I'll be good to go the rest of the way.

"No, I think I've got it."

He nods and takes off as the passenger in a car I just noticed was by the curb.

Am I prepared for the drive? Usually a road trip means that something fun is at the end, but from all the interactions I've had with my family members this week, I wouldn't be surprised if I'll have stepped into the Twilight Zone.

"This is what we're driving to the middle of nowhere?" Spencer asks when he pulls up thirty minutes later. "We might not even need a hotel room. We can just sleep in the back seats."

"There's no way I can sleep in the truck. I'll let you do that and use some money to get a motel." I glance over at the two large suitcases, a backpack and a medium-sized duffle bag he brought. "At least we'll have plenty of room to take whatever we need."

"Your requested snacks, m'lady," Spencer says, opening the duffle bag. Inside are all the things I asked for as well as what looks to be dried fruit and some nuts. Maybe that's what he prefers?

"Thank you, kind sir. Put it up front and the rest of your stuff in back. I'll finish packing and be right out." A couple of hours driving tonight will be better than waiting for the morning rush hour traffic to subside here in Boston.

Once I have everything secure, I walk over to the driver's side door.

Spencer holds out his hand and I look at it, confused. Then I reach over and slap it like a high five.

He laughs. "I'll drive."

I frown. "Um, no. Thank you for being willing to escort me home, but I'll drive."

"I've heard some things from your roommates." Spencer's voice is low, as though he's trying to whisper a secret between us, even though there's no one else outside.

"What things?" I say in the same low voice.

"That you struggle to drive."

I tilt my head back and laugh. "I struggle to drive smaller vehicles in the city, Spence. Trucks like this," I say, pointing to the beast next to us, "are how I learned to drive."

"You've seen several trucks like this?" Spencer asks.

"I mean, not several. But you have to remember that I'm from the country. I've driven in a truck that I practically needed a mini stepladder to get into. I've got this."

I slip around him and hop up into the driver's seat. When the ignition turns over, the power behind it makes me chuckle. At least Dad didn't get something that would break down on the drive. Knock on wood.

Spencer clicks his seat belt with some force, like I might actually get us into an accident. "Are you sure you can see everything? It's a big vehicle."

"Spencer," I say, glancing out the rearview mirror and through the side mirrors, "I appreciate your concern. Now let me drive."

I press the gas gently, trying to get a feel for how temperamental it is. The truck flies out of the driveway and narrowly misses a trash can on the opposite side of the street. Spencer is hanging onto the oh-crap handle with a white-knuckled grip and I try to hide my smile as I pull off down the road on the way to the interstate.

This should be fun.

11

SPENCER

There's always a first time for everything. Thinking I'm going to die within the first five minutes of being in the truck with Millie hadn't crossed my mind before.

"Are you sure you don't want me to drive?" I say again, holding on for dear life to the handle above me. "I have a few more years of experience."

She shakes her head again, and it's like I'm seeing a completely different side of her. Instead of seeming nervous, she's sitting up straight, looking more confident than I've ever seen her. And it looks good on her. Not that I should note something like that, being her brother's best friend and all, but she's very cute at this moment.

"How are we on gas?" I ask, not sure if I should judge that part of her by the way she tore out of the driveway with reckless abandon. Maybe she's one of those people who sees how close they can get to the E.

"We've got enough to get us out of the city, I think," she says, pressing the buttons on the steering wheel. The dashboard changes here and there, showing that we can go about four hundred and fifty miles.

"How big is the tank in this thing?" This vehicle had to have been made for someone in Texas. Everything needs to be big there, right?

"It's probably sixty to seventy gallons for that much left."

I turn and study Millie, watching as she changes lanes every once in a while, a little jerky, but there are no crunch sounds. Maybe the size of this beast distracts drivers and they're steering clear.

"How do you know so much about trucks?"

She chuckles and says, "Just a lot of experience with them."

She's focused on the road and while there's a comfortable silence between us, I don't know if I can keep that going for thirty plus hours.

The sun is still high in the sky, but I'm wondering how long of a stretch of driving I should prepare myself for. "Are we driving through the night? Or what's the plan?"

"I was thinking about four or five hours and then we'd stop for the night. Does that work for you?"

"Sure. Do you have a hotel reservation somewhere?"

Millie turns and gives me a frown. "No. We'll just go until we're ready to be done and then find a hotel."

"Huh?" I sound like a caveman but I've never been on a trip that wasn't carefully curated with the stops and hotels picked before we left. Then again, I usually fly to my destinations.

"We'll just pick somewhere off the freeway and stay the night."

"What if the hotels are booked?"

She gives me a knowing smile and says, "Spencer. It's the middle of April. Most high school and college spring breaks are over and it's not like there aren't plenty of options this time of year. If we were leaving around Christmas, then yes, it would be better to get a reservation."

I'm shocked and trying to comprehend this move of hers. Just drive up and ask if they have a room? Two rooms, I mean.

"You've never done that before?" she asks.

"Nope. I usually book online so I have one less thing to worry about."

Millie laughs. "I knew you were on top of things, but I didn't realize it was out of worry. That gives me a new perspective on you."

I shake my head and stare at the traffic ahead of us. What is something we can talk about so I'm not worrying about her driving or where we're going to stay the night?

"Did you ever get a message from your ghost date?"

She frowns and shakes her head. "No, but apparently he's still in my top three guys I've matched with, so that just goes to show you how well I do in the relationship department. Maybe I should become a nun. No, a hermit in a cottage in the forest."

"As an extreme extrovert, with rare introvert tendencies, I think I'd rather die."

We both laugh and it's a fun, relaxing moment.

"I don't know. I don't think there's any fixing me." Millie's expression is serious and I wonder what examples her brain is pulling up for her to think like that. Hopefully it's not just from one guy who didn't show up.

"You'll be fine. It's not like you're eighty and still single."

She's silent for a long moment and says, with a horrified expression, "You think I'll be eighty before I find the love of my life?"

I turn to look at her, surprised she took it that way. "No, that's not what I meant. But now I'm curious. Do you have a particular list of traits you're aiming for? James-specific. perhaps."

"His name is Jordan. Did anyone tell you that you're awful at remembering names?"

"Maybe. So, your list?"

"No. I have a fear that I won't have thought it through

completely and that whatever I manifest to the universe will be not quite what I pictured."

Her words cause me to laugh so loud and long that I'm slapping my knee, which makes me think I'm turning into my old man.

"I'm sorry, I don't know why I thought that was so funny. I guess we should start at the beginning. What is the hardest thing for you to do when talking to someone you're interested in?"

"You at least know how to talk to other women. I can't talk to an attractive male to save my life. Unless he's someone I've known for a long time." She gives me a small smile.

Talking has never been a weak point for me, so maybe I could help her.

"Doesn't the matchmaking app have classes on that kind of thing you can take?" I say, remembering something about it when my friend Miles was going through it with me. I only half-listened at the time, but maybe a class could help her.

I open the app and glance around, realizing that I'm logged into her profile still from the diner. At least this gives me more access to the app.

"Yeah, here it says there are several options of in-person or online classes you can take for various personality classes, hobbies, etc."

Millie frowns and says, "Personality classes? That makes me sound like a dysfunctional robot."

"I promise, I didn't mean that."

She's quiet for several moments and then says, "What if you coach me on it?"

"On what, exactly?" I ask, not sure I like this line of questioning.

"You know a lot of things about the dating world that I can't even comprehend. And I trust you. Will you help me on the aspects that go into being a normal human being on a date?"

"I'm not the best example of relationships either. What's your biggest hope?"

"To walk into a room confident that I should be there and that if I want to approach someone, I won't run from the room in terror."

"It's that bad, huh?" I say, trying to keep my expression neutral. She looks serious as all the words come out.

She shrugs. "Worse."

"Why do you have a hard time with Tara? And what's with the guy your mom talked about on the phone as bringing a plus one? Jonathan? John?"

"Jordan."

I wait for her to say something, anything to explain who the guy is to her, but it seems she won't confess without some prying.

"Did something happen between you and Jamison?"

Millie sighs and turns to glance at me before focusing on the road again. "He was someone I liked throughout high school."

"Did you ever date?"

The truck jerks to the right and I'm grasping for my favorite handle right now as we hit the gravel on the side of the freeway. Millie rights the truck and continues on.

"Did you see the large animal on the road?" she asks, giving me a small smile.

"That's a good question. No, I didn't."

"Well, I just saved your life."

Point taken. Leave the dating questions for later on this trip.

12

MILLIE

The layers I'd built around me after years of the crazy, the drama, the overwhelming disappointment that was my life living back in northeastern Colorado, well, they're losing their strength. I can't just head back and do the same thing I've always done with my family.

I've learned things, and even if they've changed somewhat, I'm not sure they'll be extra happy about me wanting to be free on the east coast.

"I won't kill us," I say. I swerved the truck on purpose. There's no way I want to talk about the trauma of the Sweetheart's dance junior year. I'd actually been asked to dance by someone not related to me, which is hard to do in a town as small as Bitter Springs. It was one of Jordan's friends and I was so excited that I'd be in the same group Jordan was for this dance. Maybe I could do or say something that would show him how cool I was and he'd want to date me.

I never got out more than a hello the entire night. Jordan's date would be his girlfriend the rest of that year and the guy who'd taken me out avoided me until graduation.

"What about your dating life?" I dare to ask. "You seem like you could use a steady girlfriend about now."

Spencer laughs. "Well, if we make it through this trip alive, I might have to reconsider it."

"What's been your longest relationship?" I ask.

"Six months, I think. That was a while ago, though."

"So, why the constant change of women?"

Spencer takes a moment to mull that over. "I'm not sure. We just hang out for the time needed and then move on to other things. I rarely lead them on."

"What about your newest gal? The one who broke up with you?"

He frowns. "She was ready to be serious and put a label on our relationship. I wanted to wait."

"To see if things actually worked out? Or are you scared of relationships?"

"I'm not scared. I'm just not ready. It's hard to know what I would like in a woman if those qualities on the checklist change from week to week."

"You might as well create your own woman if you're trying to get all the same qualities into one body."

His expression shows he doesn't like that answer. It's fleeting, before he reaches over and presses several buttons on the large screen that control everything from music to the warmth of the seats.

"How about we get some music going?" He finds a station that plays some of the new pop hits but there's a hint of static every four or five beats and it's going to drive me insane.

"Do you not listen to the radio?" I ask. I lean over and turn the tune button until it lands on one of the normal Boston stations.

He gives me a sheepish grin. "I usually listen on Spotify."

"And what do you listen to?" I ask, turning down the volume a couple of notches.

"It depends on my mood, to be honest. Sometimes I need classical music and other times I need something with a beat."

"Or something with a story to it that you can picture yourself a part of?" I say, thinking about all the times I'd driven in the little beater car I'd had in high school, with the music turned up and me singing at the top of my lungs.

Spencer bobs his head back and forth as if trying to decide. "I guess that happens when I listen to country, but not that often."

"Connect your phone. I don't think we'll have clear service on the radio stations for a while."

"Do you want me to put the map up too? So we know where we're going."

I laugh again, and it only gets worse when I see the confused expression he's sporting.

"I've driven to Boston and back a couple of times. There aren't too many turnoffs."

"You don't want to see the progress? We could see the estimated time of arrival and try to beat it." He looks so hopeful and I can't help but nod.

"Okay, if you need something like that to get us through."

He presses a bunch of buttons and finally connects his phone to the truck's speakers. What sounds like the beginnings of a movie plays and I try to figure out what it's from. The title and track aren't displayed on the screen, since he wants to see the map.

"What's this from?" I ask, curious.

"*The Man from Snowy River*," he says.

With a grin, I nod, recognizing it now. It's been some years since I've seen the movie, but the album is good.

"Do you listen to a lot of musical scores?" I ask.

"When I need to focus, yes. But I like a good range of music, so I don't listen every day."

"What about Disney songs?"

He chuckles. "I don't know if I'm totally versed in those. I didn't have any siblings, so I feel like I missed out on a lot."

"Well, what if we do a musical trivia? Find a playlist of songs we might know and we'll see who knows the titles the fastest."

Spencer nods with a smile. And there goes that surge of attraction again. I'm going to need to put on the metaphorical brakes because we're going to be spending a lot more time together on this trip. I've spent the last five years daydreaming about Jordan, but why does my mind not hold on to that like it did a few days ago?

13

SPENCER

I'm not used to being called out by anyone, let alone someone who I just volunteered to be her date to her brother's wedding. She thinks I'm an expert at dating, whereas it always feels like I'm seconds away from an explosion of sorts.

There, I said it. I have commitment issues.

I've been through a lot in life, and I try to be positive about it. But when you've pledged your whole soul and the future of your life to one person, you want that to be taken seriously and not just thrown out with last year's styles.

My parents had their own struggles, and it was difficult to watch them rebuild their marriage after what should've been a happy time. My father stepped out on my mother for a few months, fulfilling the cliche of being with his receptionist.

Why my mother gave him a second chance, I'm not sure. I don't know if I would've had the strength to do something like that. And so I date. A lot. Knowing that if I don't get too close, I can't get hurt. That I'm the one doing the leaving and not the other way around.

My mother cried tears for weeks, and while I try to be as

emotionally unfeeling as my father used to be, I think I'd be a crier.

Their marriage is stronger than ever now, and they are always doing something with one another, aside from Dad's golf habit. But I don't want a repeat. What if the person I love doesn't love me as fiercely as I love them?

And that, ladies and gentlemen, is why I continue to mingle.

We're listening to a random mix of nineties pop and the newer phase of country music, all of which are on a playlist created by Millie. I'm surprised at the variety in her musical tastes.

It's long past dark when we decide to pull off the freeway and find a hotel.

"Let's stay there," Millie says, pointing to a one level rambler-like building. The neon lights are mostly burned out, to only say "Vaca" which I think means cow in Spanish. I can only remember a handful of words from the classes I took on set.

"Are you not worried about the conditions inside when it looks like it's abandoned on the outside?"

"Considering it's under a hundred dollars, I think I'll survive eight hours."

I've never thought of myself as prudish, but I'm a little nervous about the look of this hotel.

Millie walks in and asks for two rooms, refusing to accept any payment from me.

"You just paid for my new phone," she says. "The least I can do is pay for your hotel room tonight."

I've already looked up on the website to see if there is one of the chain hotels under my father's firm close by, but there's nothing. Will I die tonight? Probably not. Will I actually sleep? Also no.

The physical room keys are not the cute, intricate metal

kind from an old Victorian Mansion. It's a basic metal key with a colored tag attached, but they're covered in grime.

"Which way is it?" I ask, taking the key from the clerk while Millie holds the other.

"Out the door and the third and fourth doors to the left." The clerk settles back into the seat and stares at his phone again. I'll take that as my cue to leave.

There are a few lights that illuminate the parking lot and a few overhead lights as we walk over to our rooms, but it's very dark where we end up.

"What time are we leaving in the morning?" I ask, dropping off Millie's bag next to her. I take a few steps to my door and fumble with the key, trying to get it into the lock.

"Early. Six or seven?"

"Sounds good. I'll set an alarm."

"Good night," Millie says. I open the door and am hit with the smell of something rotten. I'm about to search for whatever critter might've died in here until I hear Millie shout something.

"What's wrong?" I ask, peeking my head out the door. While I have my head sticking out there, I breathe in the refreshing air.

She looks like she's frozen, slowly raising her arm to point into her room. I walk over to see what she's seeing.

In what should've been a fully furnished room, it's completely empty. The walls have lines where there used to be art of some kind on the wall. They even took the smoke detector. Who they are, I'm not sure, but I can't believe this.

"Well, maybe they're remodeling?" I say, already turning to walk back to the front desk.

Once inside, the man behind the counter looks up, irritation etched all over. "No refunds."

"Are you serious right now? The room you assigned to my friend is completely empty."

He narrows his gaze at me and says, "How is it empty?"

I have to take a deep breath and say, "That's why I'm here. There's no bed, no lamps, not one scrap of fabric in the entire room."

"We fine people who take stuff from our rooms."

"I'm sorry, Gary, is it? We just barely got the keys from you less than five minutes ago. You think we'd be able to empty an entire room in that amount of time? That's only possible with a Harry Potter wand."

Gary looks appalled. "Harry Potter would never use his precious magic on something like that."

Um...that didn't go as planned.

"Will you at least come look?" I wave for him to walk out the door with me.

He grumbles the entire way and then frowns when he looks inside the room. "I'll have to call the police on you."

That shakes Millie out of whatever trance she's been in. "Police? We just checked in."

I shake my head, trying to tell her without words that we'll just have to ride this one out.

Gary calls someone and within a minute, a cop cruiser pulls up. Out steps a man almost a foot taller than me. How does he fit behind the wheel?

"I was called for a theft?" The cop points a flashlight at me and then Millie, studying us.

"Oh, hey, Kurt," Gary says. "We've got these two for theft of everything in this room."

Cop Kurt takes a few steps toward us and finally drops the flashlight. "You emptied the contents of this room?"

"No. We just got here," Millie says. "We checked into two rooms and I opened this one and saw there was nothing inside. Spencer went into his and, well, I'm not sure what he found."

"My room seemed normal, except it smelled like something died in there."

"They're the ones who took the bed and everything, Kurt," Gary says, pointing at us like we're in the middle of a childhood tattle session.

Kurt looks around the parking lot and then back to us. "What vehicle are you driving?"

"The beast," Millie says, pointing to the large truck.

"Do you mind if I look inside?" Kurt asks, looking over at me.

"I don't mind, but it's her father's vehicle."

Millie walks over and opens the door to the front seat and then keeps walking, opening every door and even the back tailgate.

Kurt peeks in and checks inside the passenger side doors. Once he gets around to the back, he asks, "What's the gas mileage for something like this?"

"Probably ten miles to the gallon," Millie asks, looking confused.

I'm just as baffled. He's asking about a truck when he should investigate a theft, which we obviously didn't do.

"Aren't you going to arrest them?" Gary asks.

Shaking his head, Kurt says, "No. They've done nothing wrong. Massachusetts plates and they've got luggage in the back seat, meaning they've been traveling for a while. There isn't anything in here that would belong in one of your rooms."

"So what am I supposed to do, then?" Gary asks.

"Call your manager and let him know they'll have to file an insurance claim."

Gary's face falls. He turns to walk away, but before he goes, I hear him say, "I'm so getting fired for this."

"Hey, what about another room?" I ask.

"We don't have another one available."

I glance around and see at least fifteen doors in the place. "You only had two rooms available to rent?"

"The others haven't been cleaned in a few weeks. After this,

I don't want to get into more trouble with a one-star review from you all."

I walk over and pick up Millie's small duffle bag. I take it to the truck and throw my own in the back as well. "Let's go."

"We paid already," Millie says. Her expression makes her look like she's debating what to do with the whole situation.

I chuckle and say, "If we stay here, we'll be sleeping on the floor or in a room that might kill any sense of smell I have. Let's go find somewhere else to sleep." I'll give her the money she spent just to get us away from this place.

This time she hands over the keys. I start the vehicle, trying to settle into the seat and get acquainted with the buttons. I'm not used to something this big, as the car I drive when I need to head outside the city is a compact luxury version instead of what feels like a tank. We're not staying here though, so I'll be okay for a few blocks.

I stop in the parking lot of a grocery store. "We'll get a couple hours of sleep and then head out. I'll make a reservation along the way, so we've got somewhere to sleep tomorrow night."

Millie groans in the seat next to me. "I still owe you, though. I'm never going to be able to pay you back if you keep shelling out money like it grows on trees."

"You don't have to pay me back. This is just what I do for friends."

"A lot of good that did you with Beau. He used you and left."

Her words irritate me. Sure, I'm a little too trusting at times, but I want to share what I have, not be a hermit who never gives or serves others. And there's something about Millie that keeps pulling me in, like I'll be forever happy if I just hang out with her.

"I have a feeling you won't do the same."

14

MILLIE

Sitting in the passenger seat of the beast, I'm surprised at how vulnerable Spencer looks right now. He's so giving that he probably didn't realize what Beau did to him until I pointed it out. This is why I keep my thoughts to myself. Being blunt only hurts people.

We walk into the store a couple minutes before closing time and find two lap blankets to purchase. One has llamas on it and the one I pick looks like it's straight from the 80s or 90s because it's neon everything, with several shapes, reminding me of the Saved by the Bell reruns my mom had on VHS tapes when we were younger. To be honest, she's probably still got them.

"Do you want the front back seat? Or the back back seat?" I say with a smile.

"I'll take the front back seat," Spencer says with a laugh. "Then if anyone disturbs us, I can get to the driver's seat quickly."

By the time we settle in, my mind is going a hundred miles an hour.

"Spencer?"

"Hmm?" He sounds like he's almost asleep already.

"Sorry, I'll let you rest."

"I'm good. What's up?" I hear him shift and his voice sounds closer, so he must've turned so he's facing me a bit more.

I blow out a breath and say, "Thanks. For being here."

"Of course. I mean, I have nothing to compare it to."

Laughing, I tug the blanket up closer to my chin, but it's too short and now my feet are exposed. "Well, I've never been on a road trip that was smooth sailing, so I guess that's just the Olsen curse?"

"Being accused of emptying a hotel room in five minutes is definitely a first." We laugh and it feels good. I've been a ball of nerves since I heard Beau was getting married, and this is just the release I need.

"I can't believe they only had a few rooms to rent out."

"They obviously don't check or clean the rooms after people leave. From the smell, the room I should've been in had something dead in it for at least a month, if not more."

I shiver at the thought. It's not so much the critters that scare me, but my nose is more sensitive than most to things like that and I probably would've ended up with a migraine.

"Millie?"

"Yeah?" I'm not quite ready for sleep yet, so the continued conversation is welcome.

"Way to stand up for yourself out there."

I grin, trying to keep from sounding too pleased when I say, "Thanks."

"Just channel whatever you did when you were defending yourself when you need to talk to a guy."

Frowning, I say, "That has nothing to do with flirting or talking to a guy. I was trying not to get arrested."

Spencer chuckles and says, "True, but you were confident and wanted to be heard. There are similarities between that and getting a guy to notice you."

"So I just need to act irritated and raise my voice?"

Again I hear laughter from the front seat. "We'll work on it some more tomorrow."

It's quiet for several moments before I say, "Can we work on other stuff too?"

"Like what?"

"To be honest, I don't know. Just anything that will help me be comfortable."

"For Juaquin?"

A loud laugh escapes from me, and it takes several moments for me to calm down. I don't think I've ever met someone as funny as Spencer. It feels significant, like something I need to add to my non-existent list of qualities I like in a guy.

"Or whoever." Thoughts of Spencer have taken over the daydreams I've had of Jordan from years ago.

I'm not sure when I finally fall asleep, but I wake up to sunlight the next morning and a fading dream of Spencer dressed in a full suit of armor, walking up to a dragon who ended up having the face of Gary. Instead of a knight or damsel in distress, I was dressed more like a pageboy. I'm not going to over analyze that one.

Once I sit up and stretch, I glance over the seat to see that it's empty. What happened to Spencer?

I glance out the windows, trying to see if he's walking anywhere. Nothing.

Hopefully he didn't go too far because he has the keys to the truck. I open my duffle bag, which I used as a pillow last night. I can feel the imprint of the zipper along my jawline. That's just the cherry on top of this trip. Spencer will never travel with me again after all the mishaps.

There's a sound outside and I duck down before sitting up enough to peer out to the parking lot.

"Hey," Spencer says after opening the door. "Everything okay?"

Trying to put on a smile, I say, "It's just been a weird twenty-four hours, you know?"

He laughs and says, "That I definitely do. I wasn't sure what you'd want for breakfast, but I got some orange juice and some bagels and muffins. Are you ready to head out?"

"Thanks for that. I just need to get a couple things in the store and then we can start our quest." I wrinkle my nose. Our driving across the country is not some journey meant for fifteenth century knights.

"Do you want me to wait here?" he asks.

"Well, if you want more snacks than that, come back in." I point to the small bag of breakfast items he brought.

He raises an eyebrow and says, "What snacks?"

It's strange that I'm so used to being the naïve one that to have him be new at road trips is a mind twist.

"Anything you like. Chips, crackers, chocolate, candy, drinks. Whatever you're feeling."

Spencer frowns. "Why don't you just stop and get food on the drive?"

I hesitate, because it's been a long time since I've had that thought. "For a long drive, sometimes you need things to keep you awake while driving. Or when it gets to the boring part of the drive."

"So you eat when you're bored?"

Laughing, I nod. "On road trips, absolutely. Then we can stop later and get food, but it helps us keep going when otherwise we'd have to stop all the time. With this truck, we'll probably have to pull over for a restroom break before we need gas."

I lead him through the store, throwing a bunch of snacks into the cart. He's picked out a couple of things, but I've got a few large bottles of water, three kinds of chips, and a bag of sunflower seeds. This will add to what he got me yesterday.

"You eat those when you drive?" he asks, looking grossed out.

"Yeah, you'd be surprised how much a sunflower seed can help pass the time."

"Don't you hate the cleanup process after, though?"

I laugh and say, "I don't spit them out like I'm on a baseball field. Just grab a cup from the drink machine area over there and voila!"

Then I make my way to the women's aisle.

"What do we need here?" Spencer asks, curious.

"Um, just, these," I say, trying to be casual about adding a box of tampons to the cart. My brothers are always squeamish when they see stuff like this, but Spencer just nods.

"Do you need chocolate?" he asks, his expression filled with concern.

Laughing, I shake my head. "I think we'll be okay."

It's both weird and sweet that we're referencing my period without actually saying anything. Him not acting weirded out and trying to help gives him bonus points I shouldn't be handing out to my brother's best friend.

We buy the food. I insist on paying for his sandwich and chips. He must've been nervous I wouldn't really pull off the road for food at some point today.

I put everything in back on the driver's side before we drive again.

"Are you changing clothes?" Spencer asks. I see that he's wearing the same thing as yesterday.

"I'll just wait until we get to a hotel later tonight. Get a shower in and then relax."

"I'm paying for that one," he says, giving me a stern look like I shouldn't even argue with him.

"As long as there's furniture, I'll be okay with it."

We set out on the drive, battling each other for the radio playlists.

He's quiet for several moments and then turns to me with a hesitant smile. "Who's Jordan to you?"

"Jordan?" I say, hoping he'll think it was all made up. He actually got the name right this time.

"The one your mom mentioned."

I sigh. Why does he have to remember all the things? "He was the guy I crushed on from third grade all the way until, um, the end of high school. He was a year older than me and seemed like a great guy."

"And?" Spencer asks. I can feel his stare, but I keep my eyes focused on the road.

"And he's a nice guy."

Spencer groans. "Really? Was he the star quarterback of the football team? Or your high school royalty?"

I shrug. "He was pretty popular."

"And where did you fit in?" he asks.

I have to turn to see if he's joking or not. "Where do you think I would be?"

"From your love of numbers, I could see in a math club or something. Or you hung out with the drama kids, helping as a member of the stage crew. No, I can see you as a bookworm. You're also athletic, so maybe you played a sport in there somewhere and hung out with those kids?" He pauses and shakes his head. "Maybe you connected with several groups of people but never really got super close to any of them. Am I right?"

"I wasn't in a math club, or involved in the drama group, but I did kind of float among the groups at the school. Just not in the popular group."

"Did you want to be? In the popular group, I mean."

Several moments tick by as I analyze what thoughts to share there. "Back then, I wanted to be cool without rebelling like most of them did. I wanted to fit in because I'd longed to be at an actual school rather than what my mom called home-school. But then again, I kind of just wanted to get out of high school and move on." I turn to look at him and say, "What about you? Where did you fit in?"

He chuckles. "Well, I was valedictorian of my class, and earned the title of prom king and homecoming king."

I frown. "Of course you did."

Spencer's hand is on my shoulder and he says, "Millie, I was homeschooled."

"Wait, what? I figured you had to be through elementary school because of the show you were on, but you were homeschooled through all your years?"

He nods and says, "I was still on a few shows off and on. It would've been hard to start and stop in a traditional school, so my parents just kept hiring tutors until I was ready to apply for college."

"My mom let us go to public school in ninth grade," I say, my brain calling up the memories. "Well, when I say homeschooled, it was mostly just do whatever. I had to help with the kids a lot and then we'd go play out in the fields behind the house when I was free."

"How did you learn to read and stuff?"

I blow out a big breath. "Freshman year was really hard. I was in a lot of 'catch-up' classes. But I like to read, so it was fascinating the worlds I could read about once I learned. And I worked through the summers to make sure I wasn't behind in the other subjects."

"I can't even imagine how hard it would be to work on things that late in life." We're both silent for a while, lost in our own thoughts of the past.

We've driven for quite a while and I've even gotten Spencer hooked on sunflower seeds. It's time to stop and gas up and get a bathroom break before we keep heading west.

We spend a lot of the next several hours laughing until our stomachs hurt from a comedy station on XM Radio this truck has. Later, we were sucked into a true crime podcast on another channel that still gives me the creeps.

By the time we pull into another hotel that night, we're both exhausted. My lower back has tightened up a ton, and I'm grateful that this hotel is clean, while also having a pool and hot tub. I'll have to soak before going to bed or tomorrow the next leg of the journey will be worse.

We get to the check-in desk and Spencer begins the process for the rooms he reserved.

"I'm sorry, sir. We only have one room available."

Spencer straightens and pulls out his phone. He turns to look at me and says, "I promise I booked two rooms."

I give him a reassuring smile.

Scrolling through his emails, Spencer finds the one he needs and shows it to the clerk. "See, I booked two rooms here."

The clerk studies the email and goes back to typing away on the keyboard. "I'm sorry, sir. It doesn't show you listed here."

I lean around Spencer's shoulder, trying to be helpful.

"What's the address here?" I ask.

The clerk rattles it off. It doesn't match the one from the email.

"Are we in North Oak, Missouri?" I ask, pointing to the address so Spencer can see what I'm talking about.

"No, ma'am," the clerk says. "That's about ninety minutes north of here."

A pit forms in my stomach and I'm not sure what the solution is, especially since Spencer is the one who booked it. I don't think I have another hour and a half in me to drive tonight, though, even if Spencer takes over.

Spencer blows out a breath and says, "Do you know if there are any other hotels near here with two room openings?"

The clerk frowns and shakes his head. "I'm sorry, but we have a big convention this week and most of the hotels are fully booked."

Glancing my way, Spencer's gaze is on me and I find myself gulping as I look into his crystal blue eyes.

"What do you want to do?" he asks.

It takes several seconds for my brain to catch up, since I don't think I've ever had someone ask me something like this.

"Well, is there a way to get your money back and just stay here?" I ask. Even now, my heart is thumping at the idea we'll be sleeping in the same room. Sure, last night we slept in the truck, which is much smaller than a room, but there's something a lot more intimate about sharing a hotel room.

Spencer nods. "Are you okay sharing a room?"

I paste on a smile. "Yeah, that should be fine. We're just sleeping, right?" My cheeks burn as I think of the other possibilities that happen in hotels. And I need to move on from those impossible thoughts because I'm Beau's little sister. Spencer has called me his friend several times in the past week. I shouldn't be thinking about other options in the romance department.

The clerk processes the payment and hands us two keys.

"Room 248."

We take our luggage to the elevator.

"How much do I owe you for this room?" I ask, taking one of the key cards from him.

"I'm not telling you because you don't owe me a thing. You've paid for it with your knowledge of road tripping and snacks consumption. Are you going to use that blanket again?" Spencer asks, pointing to the blanket over my arm.

I shrug. "Yeah, I like sleeping with a blanket and forgot to pack one in the craziness of the past couple of days. The ones in the hotel aren't always comfortable. This should work for tonight."

"At least we'll be in actual beds tonight, right?"

"Yeah, for sure."

He unlocks the door and pushes it open, awkwardly trying to hold it and wave me in. I wheel my small suitcase into the room and stop, frozen. The room isn't a double queen. It isn't even a king-sized bed. But there in the middle of the room is a single queen bed, which is usually just a double at hotels. Meaning, we'll be a lot closer than we have been before.

"Everything okay?" Spencer asks from behind me.

"Um, yeah. It's great." My legs start working again and I wheel my suitcase over to the corner of the room before turning around.

Spencer freezes in the same spot I just was, looking at the small bed in shock. "I can, um, sleep on the floor."

I shake my head. "I'll sleep on the floor. You're the one who paid for the room."

"Again, you don't have to bring that up. I'm happy to help."

"Why don't we both just share it? I mean, we're only sleeping and then heading out."

He turns to study my face and says, "Are you sure you're okay with that?" When I nod, he says, "I promise this wasn't some elaborate ruse to do anything inappropriate."

I'm grateful he's a gentleman, but I also wish I was at least on the scale of being desirable to men.

"I know, Spencer. It's fine. Remember, we're friends. This works." At least it's clean and it doesn't smell. I'm guessing there are no cockroaches either. "You take the first shower."

He grabs his clothes from his bag and heads into the shower.

I slip into my swimsuit, a striped top with high-waisted flower bottoms. Thanks to Evie for that purchase, as I've only ever had one-piece swimsuits and usually a solid color, with no patterns to boast about. I forgot sandals that aren't leather and won't be ruined by water, so I still have to wear my socks and shoes to the pool. Ugh, I hate doing that, but after the events of last night's hotel debacle, there's no way I'm walking to the pool barefoot. I've seen too much.

It takes about five minutes for me to settle into the hot tub, and in that time, another woman comes to join. There are three kids in the pool, and their father is throwing them a football while they jump in to catch it before it hits the water. I have a great view of it, laughing along with the kids as they are successful or need to try again.

"They look like wonderful kids," the woman says, pointing to the water.

I grin. "Yes, they do."

"Oh, are they not yours?" the woman asks.

Laughing, I say, "No, definitely not mine. I'm just trying to soak after a long day in the car."

"I understand that, dearie. We are heading for a wedding back in Idaho and I'm just wishing we'd been able to fly."

I try to keep a smile on my face as she continues to speak. Flying hasn't been on my wish list in years.

The door to the pool opens. Spencer is there, his eyes wide but his shoulders sagging with relief.

"What's wrong?" I ask.

He walks over and squats down next to me. "I just wanted to make sure you're okay. You weren't in the room when I got out."

"No, I just needed to relax some muscles."

"That's not a bad idea. I might go get my swimsuit on."

"Yes, please do," the woman in the corner of the hot tub purrs.

Spencer gives me a look that I've learned to read as his "Did that really just happen?" face and says, "I'll be right back."

Once he's out of the room, the woman scoots closer. "I see. You've chosen a much more handsome guy than I originally thought."

"We're just friends. Driving to the same wedding."

"So you understand how I feel. Weddings can be so exciting, but sometimes they're the worst. And I have a feeling this time it's going to teeter on the rough side."

"Why do you say that?" I probably shouldn't be egging on this lady who seems prone to gossip, but I'm always interested in hearing about a good train wreck. Not the actual variety, but the kind that you can see between people a mile away.

"I'm the aunt to the bride and she's had an up and down kind of life. She's learned a lot over the years, but I'm a little worried because she's getting married so quickly. They've only known each other for a handful of weeks. Is that enough time to know someone before you commit your entire life to another person?"

I'm not sure how to answer that one. It should probably come from someone who's had over ten failed dates in their life.

Spencer comes in and slides into the hot tub, making strange sounds as he tries to acclimate to the water temperature.

"So, are you escorting your girlfriend to a friend's wedding?"

Spencer makes that face again and something about it makes me wonder if it's because she just called me his girlfriend. I don't look like any of his past dates or girlfriends, but why do I wish I held the title of romantic interest at least? Is it I want to be a girlfriend to someone in general or to Spencer?

"We're heading out for her brother's wedding. I'm the best man and Millie is the sister of the groom." He turns to me for confirmation on that and I just smile weakly. Any thoughts of my brother marrying Trina Burkhead cause my stomach to tighten with anxiety.

"How wonderful. You two make a great couple. I could picture you both doing that over there?" She's pointing to the kids now, the father throwing out several toys and diving for them.

"What do you mean?" I ask, trying to figure out her thinking.

"Creating children and then enjoying some time together in

the pool." She gets out of the hot tub with a wink and grabs a towel from the shelf to dry off with.

I have to bite my upper lip to keep from giving her a look of "Are you serious?" There's no way I can even look at Spencer right now. We've been talking about so many things in relationships and he probably thinks I'm a crazy girl who struggles with life. He's not wrong.

"I don't know about that," I finally say.

"You don't want kids?" Spencer asks, surprise in his tone.

"I want kids, just not while I'm drowning in school and life. I don't think I'd be the best role model."

Spencer shakes his head. "I didn't know you long before you quit working as a nanny for that one family, but it seemed like they were the most normal when they were with you."

"I don't know if I'm just burned out from having to raise my siblings and then doing that as a job, but I think I need a few more years before I make a final decision about having kids."

"What makes you hesitant?" His question is so earnest.

Here's another bridge I have to either navigate under or over. Am I going to avoid talking about it so Spencer doesn't have the horrible feelings about me that many people in my family have?

He's so patient, watching me as I mull over everything.

"I love my parents in their own way, but it's hard because I don't feel like they ever really parented me. I had to watch how other people would parent at parks and shops and other social situations and then put that into practice for my younger siblings. I don't have a typical sister-brother relationship with them because they would always go back to our parents and get whatever they wanted when I said no. That's why I quit nannying. I deserve to at least have the support of someone when I'm taking care of children."

"You don't think the future man of your dreams could help you through those times? To back you up on your decisions?"

I open my mouth to respond. The easiest answer would be no, because I've never seen an example like that. Definitely not my father or my uncles. "Is there really someone out there who could do that?"

I've revealed way too much of myself on this trip, and I don't know if I can close Pandora's box now.

The water is making my skin itch, so I stand and walk over to get a towel.

Spencer is lost in thought, still in the hot tub. When I wrap the small towel around most of me, he glances up.

"I think if you want someone like that, Millie, you'll find him. If you can't find exactly who you want, there are plenty of men who are able to be trained."

I smile, not sure what to make of that statement. All my dating experiences so far have been awful, and I've always said luck wasn't on my side. But the way Spencer says it, I can almost believe him. Almost.

15

SPENCER

I must've lost some cells that control common sense over the course of the last day. Nothing has been as expected and it's like my body and mind are rebelling against the regularly scheduled programming.

Maybe the entire atmosphere at the hotel had done things to make life awkward, but I was worried when I couldn't find Millie in the room.

Sitting with her in the hot tub and listening to the woman talk about what a cute couple we make, it made me look at Millie a bit differently. I've thought of her as Beau's little sister for months now, trying to treat her how I would if I'd had a sister. But this is the first time I've seen her as something more than that. Which is not good, seeing as how we'll be sharing a bed tonight. Completely clothed and with pillows and blankets in between, but still.

I climb out of the hot tub and we head back up to the rooms, shivering in our wet suits.

"What are your plans now?" I ask, kind of hoping to know a schedule before I freak out again. Not that I'm turning into a stalker, but I doubt I could show up to Beau's wedding if something happened to his little sister.

"I think I'll shower. We can watch a movie."

Grinning, I nod. "Sounds good. I can order some food if you want."

"Isn't room service really expensive?" she asks, looking at me as though I have a plague of sorts.

"I'll just have pizza delivered or something. What do you like?"

"Ham and pineapple."

I freeze and stare at her. "I'm sorry, what? Fruit on pizza. That's breaking several laws."

Millie shakes her head and uses her palm to push me back a step, making the spot where she touched react and wake up all the nerve endings. "It's good. Besides, tomatoes are technically a fruit, right? They have seeds."

My mouth is open a second as I think about what she's saying. I have definitely heard the debate on tomatoes being a fruit for that reason, but never in the pineapple on pizza debate.

"I stand corrected. But we might have to make a hard line between my side of the pizza and yours."

She laughs and waves before walking into the room. I find a local pizza joint and order it while she's in the shower. I debate whether to shower, since I already tested it out before, but the chlorine is making my skin itchy.

Millie doesn't take too long and I hurry in to rinse off and get back out before the pizza comes. I'm in and out in a few minutes, but I'm trying to decide what to wear. I only brought up one of my pieces of luggage, which makes me look crazy since Millie is only carrying a small duffle bag to our hotel destination rooms. Most of my shorts and pajama pants are in the other suitcase, and I really don't want to head down there.

After donning a pair of jersey type shorts with pineapples on them, I laugh at the joke there.

"So you'll wear pineapples but not eat them?" Millie says with a laugh.

"Something like that," I say, staring at the bed. She's standing in front of it, pulling a brush through her hair with one hand and changing the channels with the other hand. "Uh, which side do you want to sleep on?"

She stops and turns. "Good question. I can sleep on either side."

"Okay, how about you go on the right and I'll go on the left?"

"Perfect." She turns around and keeps searching for something to watch, but I'm over here struggling to comprehend basic functions. Why? Because this is Beau's sister and I shouldn't be enjoying the way her hair smells like a tropical drink or the memory of how she looked in a swimsuit.

I've only just sat down on the bed when there's a knock at the door. We do a little dance, accidentally stepping in the same direction when trying to get past each other. Once I've tipped the delivery guy, I bring the pizza in and set it on the small desk next to the tv.

"Dinner is served," I say, and it's the most normal sounding thing that's happened since we got back to this room.

She chuckles and walks over to put her brush back in her bag. "You make it sound so fancy."

"Well, I've been driving with this woman who refuses to stop for proper food along the drive. So I'm sure she's hungry for something other than sugar and salt."

"I'm game for pizza anytime. Go sit on the floor and we'll eat it."

Her words pique my interest. "Don't you eat food on your bed?"

She laughs. "No. I'd rather not be swimming in crumbs the entire night."

"That was obviously a trick question, but you passed with flying colors."

She disappears into the bathroom, and I turn on the TV, changing it to the *Pirates of the Caribbean* movie I found on a channel.

"Oh, I love these movies," she says, taking a seat next to me on the floor. We're leaning our backs against the bed. I open the pizza box between us and take a slice of the meat lover's side. She picks up a piece of her fruity pizza and does a bop with her hands, as if we're supposed to toast with pizza. The gesture makes me laugh way too hard.

"What?"

"This is fun. I'm glad you invited me on this trip," I say.

"Me too," she says. "Did you watch a lot of movies and shows when you were younger?"

Shaking my head, I say, "My parents wouldn't let me watch any of *The Bright Years* while I was filming it. I kind of wish they had, so I could've seen a few quirks I might've been able to fix earlier on."

"That's interesting. How did you know how to act while watching nothing on it?"

"Practice. And there are a lot of coaches on set to help with any little thing. Dialects, where to stand, dancing coaches."

"How did you take the fame as such a young star?"

I smile. "To be honest, my parents were a huge reason I'm the semi-normal person I am today. They shielded me from a lot of the media, and I never read articles or criticism about a project I'd been on until it had been out at least six months to a year. They just wanted me to live my life without the anxiety that comes with the pressure from outside sources."

"I can imagine that's a lot. I wouldn't even know where to start with celebrity status. Wasn't that intimidating for you?"

Shaking my head, I say, "Not really. I started the show when I was four and didn't know any better."

"So regular life must've been a shock."

"Oh, yeah," I say, emphasizing the words. "It was like I'd had to relearn everything about social etiquette again. That's why I've always felt indebted to Beau and Jack. Going to college was a big change for me and they helped me through it."

We turn and watch some of the movie. It's at the part where Captain Jack Sparrow is storming down the beach looking for rum.

"What do you think about this journey? How much longer do we have?" It's been fun, but I'm kind of sick of being stuck in the truck for so many hours. It's like we need to get out every couple of hours just for me to feel some sort of freedom.

"We'll get there tomorrow night. Are you getting sick of me?" she teases. She takes a bite of her pizza and grins at me.

"No, I always enjoy hanging out with you. It's just hard watching nothing but cornfields for miles."

She grimaces. "Sorry to tell you, but it only gets worse the closer we get to home. My parents live in an area that is flat and extra dry, although it might not be too bad right now since it's spring."

She lifts a napkin to wipe at her mouth but doesn't quite reach a spot on her cheek.

"You missed a spot," I say, trying to gesture for her. She wipes again and then looks at me for another response.

I lean over and wipe it with my thumb, not realizing until I touch her skin how electrically charged this situation is. There's something about her bright green eyes that pulls me in, making me question so many things right now.

Millie clears her throat, which ruins the trance that held me to that moment.

"Uh, sorry, I, uh, just wanted to help."

She nods, looking like she's unsure about something. In a

quick move, she leans back against the foot of the bed and directs her gaze to the TV.

I'm not sure what's going through me right now, what disrupted the whole fun part of the night, but I have a feeling things are changing. And I don't know whether that's good or bad.

Once we finish the pizza, we do the awkward dance around the bed. Millie gets in first, pulling the covers to her chin. Am I supposed to sleep on the outside of the covers to be a true gentleman? I've never been in a situation like this.

The blanket we bought yesterday won't cover me even if I'm curled in a ball next to her, and it's already cold in here, which is just how I like it as long as I have a blanket.

Millie is turned over on her side already. The lamp next to her is off.

"Uh, good night," I say, pulling up the covers and sliding in. I position myself on the very edge of the mattress and that I'm not tugging on the covers at all. I place the small blanket over the top, sealing off the crack of air I can feel from not having the duvet that goes to the bottom of the bed.

I'm not sure whether this night will be better or worse than sleeping in the truck, but I'm exhausted. If I can just stay in this position for the next eight hours, I think I'll be fine.

16

MILLIE

I wake up the next morning with a crick in my neck. I've got just the top of the blanket covering me at this point. Hot air is touching my face at intervals and I turn to see Spencer's arm slung across me and the two of us in the middle of the bed. It's all very innocent, and he looks adorable sleeping there.

Taking a few moments, I study his face, trying to put together all the pieces of information he's shared on this trip. He's one of the nicest guys I've ever met. He should've been taken off the dating market years ago.

I replay the last couple days in my mind and realize the memories I have of Jordan haven't popped up nearly as often as I used to replay them. Maybe it's because Spencer is here and I have a lot more than just three memories of him at this point. It would be easy to reach over and kiss him right now, but would that break the friendship tightrope we've got going on?

Back to reality. I'd rather not wake him and break this spell. We've still got at least eight to nine hours of driving ahead of us and I'm ready to get it over with, even if that means I'll have to deal with my family. Might as well start soon.

Why do I feel so comfortable here? Is this why people are always pushing others to be in a relationship?

I reach up and run my hand through his hair, surprised at the softness of it. He inches closer, as if not wanting me to stop, but he's still asleep. What would it be like to wake up like this every day?

My phone vibrates in my pocket, and I dig it out. I must've forgotten to charge it last night and the battery's almost dead. I silence the alarm and glance over at Spencer, not really wanting to get up but knowing we've got to get on the road.

It's almost seven in the morning, which in this time zone translates to eight in the morning in Boston. We'll be crossing one more time zone today when we finally end up in Bitter Springs. My stomach tightens and twists at the thought.

I love my family, but I'm not a fan of going through everything I've been able to work on over the past four years. Hopefully we can make it through this week unscathed. And I don't want this time to end with Spencer. He's the sounding board I need and the way he's supported me, especially coming on this trip and helping me get a new phone, has been unmatched in my life.

And I think my feelings for him are crossing from brotherly to crush level.

It takes a few moments to slide out of our sleeping position without waking Spencer, but I make it to the bathroom. My hair looks like I'm Medusa since I never got around to drying it last night.

I search for a hair tie, taming it into a twisted ponytail as much as possible. We need to get on the road soon, and I don't want to mess with the frizz right now.

By the time I change my clothes, Spencer is sitting upright, rubbing his eyes. He glances around the room and gives me a shy smile when he sees me. "Uh, sorry. I guess I slept in."

"You're good. We were both tired from the drive and not sleeping the night before. Do you feel better now?"

He rubs the back of his neck and nods. "I'll go get changed and then we'll head out. Sorry about making us leave late."

"You're good," I say, throwing my dirty clothes into the bag. That he's apologetic is a bonus. My family is firmly in the always late category, but they never attempt to be on time. Which is why I hate that I'm just hurrying to get there when they've asked. Mostly, I can't keep traveling for too long because I don't have the money to squander on it. My savings needs to last me until I find a better job while still going to school.

We grab a bagel and muffin from the continental breakfast at the hotel and then head out.

Music permeates the cab of the truck and the two of us are silent for a while.

"Man, I'm tired," Spencer says, trying to stretch his long limbs inside the truck.

"Me too. But we can make it."

"How about we switch driving today?" he says. "We'll take turns when we get tired."

I shrug, trying to play it off like it's not a big deal. "I just want to be done driving the beast and trying to find parking for it. The nice thing about getting closer to my childhood town is that there is plenty of room for a vehicle like this."

"What are you looking forward to the most from this wedding?"

It's a good question, but I have to take several moments to think about my answer. "Having my rent paid for six months." I laugh, but Spencer looks like he's trying to figure something out.

"So there's nothing you want to do or see? No old haunts you've missed and want to visit when you get there?"

"Ruby's diner is one of my favorites. I haven't thought about it like that." The last time I came home was two years ago for Christmas. I'd had to sleep on the couch for a week straight because of all the relatives staying at the house, and then I drove home two days after the holiday. Once I moved into the Spice House, I'd sold that car, which helped get me another cushion in my bank account.

"Okay, so you want to hit Ruby's diner. What else is there that you've missed doing?"

"Bowling, the drive-in movie theater–"

"Those are still a thing?" Spencer asks, giving me a strange look.

I nod. "Out here, absolutely. It's so fun to grab a beanbag chair and a bunch of blankets and head out to watch a double feature. Have you ever been to one?"

Spencer shakes his head. "No, I thought those were relics from the sixties."

"Well, then we'll have to make a list of things for you to do, too. Camping, maybe?"

He chuckles. "I'm willing to do a lot of things outside my comfort zone, but I didn't really pack anything that screams ready for camping. Maybe we'll take a camping adventure when we get back to Boston. I've heard there are a lot of great places in the northeast to do that."

"I'm surprised you've never been camping," I say. "I thought that was a typical rite of passage for every young child."

"Well, my character on screen went camping, but we did a lot of work on movies and TVs in the summers, which made it hard for us to get away to camp. My mom's not the biggest outdoorsy person either, so I think that contributed to it."

"Okay, so we'll put camping on your list of things to do this year. There's a really cool spot up in Maine I've wanted to try. I'll make sure you get to experience the drive-in while we're out here, though. I hope they have one of the newer movies out. Bitter Springs is behind on a lot of things."

We drive along, listening to songs again.

"Do you want another night in a hotel? Or should we just push through?" I ask Spencer once we're two hours into the drive.

"Don't go adding more days to this trip. It's been real, it's been fun, but it hasn't been real fun."

We both laugh and I take a second to see his expression. How the guy can always be so upbeat is something I've never seen before. Even after his latest lady friend broke up with him, he'd cheered me up instead of the other way around.

I say, "Yeah, we'll be fine. We just need to stop for gas and food and then I think we can make it to my parent's house around six or seven tonight."

"Let's do it then."

The drive is filled with several hours of quizzing games, trying to figure out what the song is before the other person. At one point, the song is classical, and we're just listening as I drive.

"Why are you so against the Love, Austen app?" I ask, surprising Spencer and myself.

After getting over his shock at my question, he blows out a breath. "Says the woman who's used it once." I laugh at that. My failed attempt to use the Love, Austen app allowed me another opportunity to hang out with him.

He glances around and then back at me. "I guess it means I've failed if I have to resort to something like that."

"Not necessarily. I think you've only failed if you don't try, if you don't give it your all." Of course, I have no experience to back things up, but even though I struggle, I'm still going to try. I want to walk through life next to someone I love and who loves me back. Sure, it might take me another ten years for that to happen, maybe twenty, but I'll figure it out.

I can feel his eyes on me and I glance over, trying to read his expression. His eyes are glazed over, as if his mind is somewhere else. I'm about to break the silence, trying to get the conversation back on track when he speaks.

"I guess, in a weird way, I'm worried that they'll leave me."

"Leave you? Why would anyone do that? Aside from my roommates, you're the best thing that's happened to me in years."

His eyes clear and he smiles, the action reaching all the way to his eyes this time. Dang, the guy could be a model.

"I appreciate that. You've been a much needed part of my life too these past few weeks." Again there's silence, and whatever he's feeling right now, it's seeping out into the air of the truck.

"My parents had a hard time when I was younger and almost split up. My dad was gone one morning when I woke up and didn't come back for several months, when he and my mom worked things out.

"Then I had a co-star named Scotty Duncan. He was like the older brother I never had. I wanted to be like him and tried to do everything I could to be like him. When I was sixteen, he disappeared from my life and I haven't heard from him since."

My chest tightens and I wish I could hug him. Eyes on the road are the best chance of our survival, though.

"I'm so sorry, Spencer. I didn't know."

"Now that Beau is getting married, I worry that anything I do, any success I have, will just end up with the people closest to me leaving."

"Is that why you stopped acting?"

He shakes his head. "No, I think I just got burned out. I needed something different. Something normal. That's when I enrolled in college classes and left on-stage acting behind."

"Open the app." It's more forceful than I meant it to sound, but at least I'm communicating.

"What app?"

"The Love, Austen app. It will be like a test for you to see your results and like a hope for the future."

He raises his eyebrow. "I don't know. From the guy who never showed up for your date, I'm not sure I can trust a matchmaking app."

With a shrug, I say, "I figure it can connect people with matching or complementing personalities, but after that, it's the couple who has to do the actual work. From everything I've seen over the years, keeping a relationship going is work. Some people don't like that idea because it's not 'romantic.'"

Spencer grins at me again, but I can't tell what he's thinking. In a twist, he pulls out his phone and starts taking the test. He reads off some answers and we laugh about the questions and how much they all sound the same.

"Who is Captain Wentworth?" he asks, showing me the screen once he's finished the test. There's no picture.

I shake my head. "I'm not sure. Maybe look it up?"

He does a Google search and says, "He's part of a book called *Persuasion*. Do you know what that means?"

"I haven't heard of it. I'm sure my roomies could explain."

"Who did you get?"

My mind combs through my memories and comes up empty. "I don't remember. And if your result is someone I don't know, I probably wouldn't think of it randomly either."

We don't speak for several moments, both of us lost in our thoughts. Now that he's taken the test, I'm curious if my top three matches have changed. What if I see Spencer's picture on my profile? Instead of checking, I focus on the road, knowing I need to mentally prepare myself for what's coming.

"So, anything I need to know before I get to your parents' house?" Spencer asks. A change of conversation is what I needed, but this isn't any better.

I blow out a breath, trying to figure out where to start.

"There's so much. I don't know if I'll just overwhelm you or scare you off from my family."

"Well, I like you and Beau, so it can't be that bad, can it?"

I let out one of those deep, throaty laughs and shake my head. "Oh, we're the semi-normal ones of the group. I have five brothers total, so four younger than me. There is usually some contraption the boys have created to try driving their motor-bikes off of or a trap to catch the latest wild animal. My mom is always in the kitchen and usually grumbles at how fast we go through groceries because of all the mouths to feed. But if she didn't cook all the time, I wonder if it would be different."

"At least you got home-cooked meals growing up. Ours were always takeout."

"But you also probably got food on set, right?"

Something passes over his expression, but it disappears so quickly that I can't figure out what it was.

"What about your dad?" he finally asks.

"He's definitely a salesman. He's been selling stuff since I can remember. They opened the car lot about fifteen or sixteen years ago, and he's been all into that ever since."

Spencer grins. "Hence the purchase of a six-door truck?"

I nod. "Exactly. Where we are, families are bigger, so this will be sold within a couple of days."

"Well, like you said, you would've liked to be an only child. I wished all the time for siblings."

"Maybe you'll marry into a family with plenty to spare." I say. My heart hurts thinking of him marrying anyone and what he'd be like as a future father.

He's my brother's best friend and after meeting my family, I wouldn't be surprised if he took the first flight back to Boston.

I take the exit. "Only an hour and a half to go and you can tell me if you're glad you're the only kid."

17

SPENCER

There are a lot of things that I can claim in my life. I'm an excellent communicator and can genuinely get along with just about anyone. Willing to try random foods, as long as they aren't still squirming, and a fan of adventure. I try to see the positive in most situations.

Currently, I'm underwhelmed.

It's not until Millie takes the exit off the freeway and starts driving toward a vast wasteland of dried shrubs and weeds that I'm kind of disappointed in the landscape. Everything is the same boring beige color and I'm missing the variety of the plants and trees in Boston. Sure, things had changed quite a bit landscape-wise as we continued to drive west, but compared to the lush foliage of the northeast, this is definitely desert.

"You grew up here, huh?" I say, scanning the horizon for anything that might catch my eye.

"Not much to look at, I know. But the land was cheaper for my parents to start their life, so this is where they put down roots."

We wind through different areas, but the landscape never

changes. There's finally a small town, with a major street that looks like it could be straight out of the Route-66 era.

"There's my dad's car lot," she says, pointing to a small square of land that has cars and trucks crammed next to each other. How was the one who parked them able to get out of them? And good luck trying to pull them out if a customer wants to take one on a test drive.

I expect her parents' home to be one of the small cottages along the street we turn down, but she keeps driving and leaves the city limits.

"So, you didn't live in town, huh?"

Shaking her head, Millie says, "No, we've still got twenty minutes."

My butt is tired from sitting for so long, but knowing we're almost done with this journey is making me think I might just survive.

I'm not sure what I thought the Olsen house would look like, but this is definitely not it. It's a long rambler, taking up what would probably equal an entire block in Boston. A few shingles are missing, and a piece of the siding is hanging by one corner.

A chain-link fence surrounds a large section of the yard and from the dogs that come barking at the side closest to us, I'm a little nervous that her family is breeding attack dogs.

Millie parks behind at least five vehicles in the driveway, but there's still room behind her for more. All the space in the world compared to the small parking spots under my apartment building.

She turns off the key but doesn't move to get out.

"Are you all right?"

She lets out a long breath and says, "I'm not sure yet."

"Okay, well, I'll just hang out with you until you know."

We sit in silence for several moments. Millie has her eyes closed. I scan the house and the surrounding stuff, surprised by all of this. Old bikes are piled with a few other machines and vehicles and what looks to be a little graveyard to the side. I grew up well-off in an area where I saw little besides people like me, so this is eye-opening.

"Do you bury your family on your property?" I ask, trying to keep my eyes from bugging out.

Millie frowns. "What?"

I point toward the little crosses in a fenced off area. "Please tell me those aren't human bodies."

She chuckles and says, "No, just our dog cemetery."

I breathe out and nod. "So, your family likes dogs."

"You could say that," Millie says. She sits forward and opens the door, jumping down from the tall seat. I follow, waiting for her to come around the front of the truck. "We'll come get our stuff later. Maybe my mom already has everything full and we'll just stay at a hotel in town."

I can tell she's internally hoping that to be true.

She walks up the front steps and knocks on the door. "You don't just walk into your own house?" I ask, confused.

"It's better this way. Then they'll wrangle the dogs so they don't attack you."

I turn to look at the fence and realize the dogs aren't there anymore. With a big swallow, I say, "I appreciate that."

The door opens just a crack at first and then swings all the way open to reveal a woman who looks just like Beau.

"You two made it! I'm so glad you didn't get into any accidents or have car trouble."

Me too, I think. I wouldn't even know how to fix the truck.

Millie opens the screen door and says, "Hi Mama." Her mother wraps her in a hug so tight that I'm getting claustrophobic standing a foot away.

When the woman finally lets go, she looks at me and says, "And you must be Spencer. We've heard so much about you over the years," she said, walking over and giving me a squeeze around the waist.

"You too, Mrs. Olsen."

"Please, call me Sharla. You're practically family here. I've got some food just coming out of the oven, so you're right on time. The boys should be back from work soon."

I frown. "What time does the lot close?"

Sharla nods. "Around eight. They also don't start work until about ten in the morning, so that makes up the difference. We've just had to get used to that, haven't we, Amelia?"

Millie's smile is wooden and she nods. It's like she's been transformed into a doll ever since we pulled into the driveway.

"Let me see, did you not bring any bags with you?" Sharla asks, glancing at our empty hands.

When Millie doesn't respond, I say, "We left them in the truck."

Sharla nods and says, "Well, let's go see where you'll be sleeping and then you won't have to move the suitcases so many times. Beau should be back soon. He had to run an errand in town."

She walks down the hall and I nudge Millie forward to get her out of whatever trance she's been in.

"Sorry," she mumbles and then walks down the hall behind her mother.

There are at least ten doors down this hallway and although most of them are closed, the ones that are open show individual bedrooms.

"I've stuffed all the boys into the bunkroom," Sharla says, pointing to a room on the right. "We've got Uncle John, Aunt Mable, and their kids in two bedrooms and then Beau is in his old room. My sewing room is so jam-packed that we don't have the chance to use it for anyone."

Then she stops and puts her hand on the doorknob of a

room, but before she twists it, Millie pushes herself in between her mother and the door.

"Spencer doesn't need to see this room. You've got another room for him, right?" Millie says between clenched teeth.

"I'll just sleep out on the couch," I offer.

"Someone else already has that–"

"Or the floor. I can do that." I don't need anyone to be awkward around me.

"We'll be driving up to Danton in two days to start the activities Beau and Trina have planned."

"So we'll be staying in a hotel up there?" I ask.

Beau walks around the corner and slaps me on the back and says, "Yeah. My in-laws have us all booked for a resort there. It's good to see you, Spence."

"You too. Congrats again. I can go get a rental car and head up there now? That way everyone can have their own space?" I say.

"Let me do that for you," Millie says, pulling the keys to the truck out of her pocket.

Beau stops her and says, "No, we'll find a spot for you. Did you bring anything less preppy to wear? We've got the family camping trip tomorrow."

I glance down at my khakis and the polo I put on this morning before we left the hotel and then back at him. Shaking my head, I say, "I didn't realize camping would be part of this wedding."

I turn to look at Millie and she mouths, "I'm sorry." I don't know what it's for, but to be honest, had I known we were camping, I wouldn't have been able to pack differently than I already did.

"We'll go search for some extras in my closet," Beau says. "I need to talk to you about a few things, since you're the best man and all."

He steers me to a room that had to be his growing up.

There's a large shelf that runs the length of the long wall and is packed with trophies and medals. Baseball and football decor hangs along the walls, making it almost seem like a younger child's room.

Beau opens the double doors to the closet and I'm surprised how he fits so many clothes into such a small space.

"How was the trip?"

"It was good," I say, smiling as I think of the random things that happened. Being threatened with arrest because of stealing stuff we couldn't have done in five minutes, and then falling asleep next to Millie in the hotel room.

Beau sits on the bed. "I can't believe Millie still won't fly. It's been like ten years and driving from Boston to here is such a waste of time. I mean, you two could've been here in about five hours instead of three days."

"It wasn't that bad. I learned a lot, and it was my first time driving cross country." I'm not sure what to do since he brought me in here to search for clothes, but he's not making a move to look for anything. "So, engaged that fast, huh? Did you date Tawnya before?"

Smirking, Beau shakes his head. "No, I came home and we just hit it off. We spent everyday together and just figured we'd get hitched sooner rather than later."

"And you got a job from her father." It's a flat statement, as I try to curb the emotions I still have from his ditching me to get married. I shouldn't be surprised, though.

"Yeah, it's entry level, but I'll be scouting for the baseball organization he owns. And if I do well, I'll be able to move up, possibly scouting for the Rockies. Trina has another sister, Elaine, and no brothers, so her dad looks at me like the heir. I'd set you up with her, but I'm not on her list of favorites now. Stealing her sister is not helping me."

I frown, trying to figure out how the guy I've known since college could be so excited about something he knows little about. He'd never talked about sports much before, but there are a couple of pictures of him on the wall as a little kid dressed in baseball gear. I would think that he'd need to have at least studied the game a lot before now to get a job scouting players, but what do I know?

"That's cool. I'm glad you're happy."

"For sure. We should double date while you're here. Trina's got a few friends we can set you up with."

"I actually told Millie that I'd be her date to the wedding."

Beau turns to look at me, turning his nose up. "Millie? Are you sure you don't want to see what the Danton ladies have to offer?"

Frustration ebbs in my chest as I say, "There's nothing wrong with Millie. She's a lot of fun to be with. And I'm sure your marrying her high school bully isn't helping her emotions."

"She'll have to get over it at some point. Trina and I are soul mates."

That's a point I can't really argue, but then again, I haven't met his fiancée.

"Just be nice to your sister, all right?"

Beau stands up and hands me a few pairs of jeans and a couple older looking t-shirts. "Try these on. I don't care if they get dirty or ruined, so they'll be great for camping."

I take the clothes and follow him to the bathroom out in the hall.

"I've got to make a phone call to my smoking hot fiancée. I'll see you in a bit when dinner is on."

I nod and shut the door, trying to shake off the ick factor of Beau talking about his future wife like that. I might not be the best one to talk, since I've dated so many women, but I've never tried to refer to them solely on looks. Has Beau been like this all his life and I just never saw it before?

18

MILLIE

I'm in the seventh circle of h-e-double hockey sticks. The only reason I now know that reference is because I've had to read about a poet named Dante for one of my core classes. And with Kenzie and Trey at the house all the time, they talk about hockey a lot.

The right thing to do is to let Spencer stay in my room. But I know that my mother hasn't changed it since I graduated high school nearly five years ago.

Do I want to expose the guy I've got feelings for to catch on to the level of nerdiness that was me as a teenager? Not really. But do I want him to be stuck on the floor or even crammed into the bunkroom with my rowdy brothers? No.

Spencer comes out of the bathroom just as I'm walking down the hall and we bump into one another.

"Sorry," we both say, chuckling a bit.

"It looks like you found some camping clothes," I say, glancing down at the pile of jeans and t-shirts in his hands.

He nods and gives me a little half-smile that sends my insides to the dance floor. "Yeah, I guess this is what I'm supposed to pack."

I use my thumb to point over my shoulder and say, "I've got your suitcase in the last room on the left."

He frowns and says, "You don't have to give me your room."

"It's fine," I say, trying to play it off. "I'm used to being in the bunk room anyway. You won't get any sleep if you stay in there and you deserve it. I know it's like a whirlwind coming here."

"Where's the bunkroom?" he asks, glancing past me at the doors down the hallway.

"Really, it's fine. We're here for one night and it will be good for me to see Eric and Frank."

"You're sure?"

I swallow hard, knowing that if there was even the most remote chance that we could be in a relationship, the sight of my room will squash that completely. "Go for it. I'm going to see if my mom needs help with anything. See you at dinner?"

He nods and smiles. "Sounds good."

Why the way he stares at me sends me into a tailspin, I'll have to analyze later. Already there's a fight in the kitchen and I have to go investigate.

Minutes pass as I navigate the culture shock of being here again. I've already been assigned one of my old jobs, which is to search for my four younger brothers, ranging from eighteen to ten. It would be easy to assume that finding them wouldn't take long, since we have all of two trees in our yard, but I swear they always find new places to hide.

I lift what looks to be an old wooden fence section out in the yard and discover a large hole in the ground.

"Get out or we'll shoot!" a voice calls from below.

It's Frank, my youngest brother and quite possibly my favorite. I'm not the mom, so I'm allowed to have favorites. He's the one I took care of for most of his first few years and the one I can joke with without fear of intense repercussions.

"Aye, then I'll have to shoot ye back!" I say in my best pirate accent.

A head pops out, with shaggy dark red hair and a toothless grin. "Millie!"

He climbs out of the hole and leaps into my arms. "When did you get here?"

"A bit ago," I say, brushing back his hair so I can see his eyes. There's a large scar on his forehead. "What happened here?"

Frank ducks back a bit and says, "Danny did it when he was trying to learn to crack his whip. Mom said it needed stitches, but Dad just super-glued it together."

"Where did Danny get a whip?"

"He saved a bunch of the pop cans and turned them in for money. Then he went to the general store in town and bought it. But it's already broken now, so he can't do much with it."

That sounds about right. Anything new in the Olsen household gets broken within the first day of having it.

"Are you excited for the wedding?" I ask.

"Eh, I guess. Mom says I have to dress fancy all day and I hate that. The shirt makes me itch all over." Sounds like the talk of a typical ten-year-old.

"You and me both. We'll have to survive it together."

The door opens to the house and Mom calls out, "Dinner's ready. Come, eat."

And then it's like an army ready for an ambush, because my other brothers appear from random hiding places around the yard and charge toward the house. "I guess I don't have to look too hard for everyone else."

"Will you sit by me, Millie? Please, please?" Frank asks with his lip jutted out.

"Of course. I wouldn't want to sit by anyone else."

Sure, there's a lot of anxiety about coming back here, but being with my youngest brother soothes some of that. I'm not sure what the week will hold, but at least I'll have time to connect with the family members who are just excited for my presence rather than what I can do for them.

19

SPENCER

We've finished dinner with most of the immediate members of the Olsen family. There was some fun banter back and forth, but I was surprised at how much they all praised Beau for everything he did and kind of pushed Millie to the side a bit.

Beau is marrying the heiress to the Burkheads. Beau sold three cars today and he'll be traveling to find future superstars. Meanwhile, Millie has kept her head down and looks like the shell of who I saw in the truck just hours before.

Of course, my being the only child means I don't always get a full family dynamic, but I would think that the parents should stop anything that divides their family.

I couldn't help watching her with her youngest brother, Frank. They kept laughing softly, whispering about something I couldn't hear. As nervous as she was to come home, I like seeing her when she's interacting with her brothers. She seems to freeze any time her parents speak.

I haven't seen Millie since after dinner, when I helped her wash the dishes by hand. Yes, I am a benefactor of privilege because I've never had to wash anything by hand, let alone the entire mound of dishes.

Millie didn't shame me for that fact, just helped me learn the order to wash the dishes in. She had to refill the sink three times to make sure everything got a good, sudsy wash and then I rinsed them, drying them off after.

I'm exhausted from the day and ready to sleep since we'll probably be going in the morning. Camping sounds like it might be fun, but my stomach is all tied up in knots. From everything I've gathered from Father Olsen, they are very much into the manly man kinds of things. I'll probably have to chop down a tree to prove my strength or drink some strange concoction to join in the ancient Olsen brotherhood or something.

I walk into the room Millie mentioned earlier, surprised at the brightness of it. The walls are a sunny yellow and there are several posters of older country artists, as well as several paintings and photos. It's a lot different from Beau's room.

At least twenty-five stuffed animals cover the bed and the bedspread is yellow with little daisies all over it. This room gives off different vibes, and I'm trying to reconcile the Millie I know with what the teenage Millie must have been like. I've never been in her room in Boston, but this isn't what I would picture.

There's a knock on the door and Millie opens it a bit more, handing me my duffle bag through the opening. "Sorry, I forgot to bring this in earlier."

"You didn't have to do that," I say, walking over and taking it from her.

She shrugs. "You're a guest here." She glances around the room awkwardly.

"So this is where you grew up, huh?"

With a forced smile, she says, "Yeah. Um, let me put away the stuffies." She walks over and swipes several of them into her arms, opening the closet and dropping them on the floor inside. It's not as packed in there as Beau's closet, but there is a long sage-green dress hanging from the rod. I can picture Millie wearing it for a dance, the color complimenting her complexion and her eyes.

"These photos are amazing," I say, walking over to one that's black and white but clearly shows the horizon at sunset. An interesting choice since the sunset usually displays so many vibrant colors.

"Thanks. I took them for a class in high school. They were some of my favorites."

"You took these?" I say, the surprise in my voice thick.

She chuckles and walks over to stand next to me, her arms folded over her chest. "Yeah. It was possibly my favorite class. The teacher helped me rent a camera, and I spent the semester all over this valley, trying to find a different angle to this desert."

"Have you taken pictures since?"

Millie shakes her head. "No, I had to give the camera back before graduation and then everything in Boston cost a lot more than I was expecting. I hope to get one someday. But thanks to you, my phone takes some great photos now."

I study her profile. She looks relaxed as she stares at the photo. This must be a passion of hers and she doesn't even realize it.

"Do you like what you're studying in school?" I ask, curious about her answer. My question pulls her out of a trance and she turns to look at me.

"Yeah. They are much needed skills for learning about money and business. I think it'll help me in the future, you know?"

I point to the photo and say, "You don't want to do this for a career?"

"Take photos? That would be fun, but I don't have the training and I doubt I'd be able to support myself, especially because I don't plan to leave the east coast."

Something about that statement gives me a sense of relief, maybe because I don't want her to leave. We've gotten so close lately and I think I'd be lost without her.

"The way you light up when you look at these, I think you should at least take a class to refine your skills."

She laughs and says, "Let me get through school first and then I can experiment with things like that." She pats me on the shoulder before turning to leave. "Boston isn't cheap."

"Thanks, Millie."

She chuckles and says, "What for?"

I smile and say, "For teaching me a lot of what I didn't know."

"Well, the adventure isn't over yet. Tomorrow you'll experience the Olsen family camping trip."

"Why a camping trip? That seems like the opposite of a typical wedding event. Did you know about it?" I ask, remembering when she mouthed she was sorry.

"I forgot about it. The last time we did this was for my aunt's wedding ten years ago. No one else has gotten married since and I didn't think it was a tradition we'd have to keep."

I nod, mulling that over. I've never heard of a family going camping right before a wedding. What happens if the wedding is in the winter?

She laughs. "Which is why it's become a family thing, because it is different. I'm not sure the real reason it started. You'll be fine. Just show them you know how to make a fire and you'll be golden."

I search every recess of my brain for any fire-making wisdom I might've stored there in the past, but I've got nothing.

Millie sees my confusion and gives me a small smile. "Let me give you a demonstration." She disappears for a couple minutes, coming in with toothpicks, cotton swabs, and a small piece of newspaper. Over the next five minutes, she shows me how to start a fire and I actually feel confident I might be able to do it if asked.

"You always say you don't know anything, but you know quite a bit," I say, twirling one toothpick between my fingers.

"Cooking, cleaning, caretaking, nature, yeah. But my social skills have never been to where people are begging me to come hang out with them." There's a vulnerability in her voice, and I can see how much she would love to just be included. With her family treating her almost as a servant, I can imagine that's been hard for her.

I reach over, taking her hand in mine and grin. "Millie, will you please come hang out with me?" I meant for it to make her laugh, but I'm hoping she'll say yes.

She glances down at our hands and then back up to give me a small smile. "Is this how you hold hands?"

I chuckle and say, "One way. There are several methods of holding hands. You can do the clasping of the hands, or inter-locking of the fingers, like this." I move my hand so all our fingers are intertwined. "There are other ways, like locking pinky fingers or something like that."

When I switch to interlock with her pinky finger, it's such a simple thing, but it feels like a big step to take in a relationship that should only be friendly. She must feel it too, because she stands quickly.

"Thanks for the information. Um, good night," Millie says, giving me a warm smile before she leaves the room.

I sit on the edge of her bed and stare at the photo again. There are so many more layers to Millie than I originally thought, and I suddenly want to be the one to peel back each layer to get to know her better. I've never been this intrigued by a woman, but Millie isn't even on the same playing field as the other women I've dated.

And I'm not sure how to feel about that just yet.

20

MILLIE

Sleeping next to Frank used to be more comfortable. When he was younger, I had to go in and comfort him when he woke up several times a night. While I started in one of the other bunks the night before, he ended up next to me after a nightmare. And after all the tossing and turning he did, I only got about three hours of sleep.

And now I'm not in the mood to go camping.

I shuffle out to the kitchen, rubbing at my eyes to combat the brightness of the lights. Of course, my mother is standing over the stove, making scrambled eggs.

"What time did you get up?" I ask, sitting on a stool on the other side of the island counter.

"About an hour ago," she says, and goes back to humming to herself. I glance at the clock on the wall and see that it's only six in the morning.

"Are you ready to go camping?" she asks after she turns off the heat to the burner and pulls the large pan over to a hot pad.

I shake my head. "When did we start that?"

"Generations ago," Beau says, walking into the kitchen with

a large duffle bag. He opens the door leading to the washer and dryer and sets the bag on top. He gives me a wide smile and I frown at him. With a wave, he disappears down the hall again. To be honest, I'm surprised he's even up before the rest of the family.

"Your grandparents started the tradition," Mom says.

"Mom, they practically lived in a campground back then. Why do we have to continue this?" I already know what's going to happen after we eat breakfast. I'll be tasked to pack food for a small army and then will spend most of the trip having to clean something.

My mom gives me a stern look and says, "Because we won't be the ones to stop such a lengthy tradition. We'll be doing it for you too, if you ever get married."

Ouch, that hurt.

"I'm in no rush," I say, grateful that it's only the two of us right now. Sure, I've had fluttery feelings about Spencer ever since we woke up yesterday morning cuddled in the same bed. But he always looks at me like I'm his little sister. He even said that back in Boston when he bought a phone for me. I'll always be in the friend zone with him.

"Who all is going to be at this camping thing?" I say, my tone still sharp.

"A bunch of the family will be there. All the cousins will be so glad to see you." My mother opens the double doors that hide the washer and dryer and starts folding clothes. Of course, she'll wash the bundle Beau just left for her without complaint.

The Olsen side of the family are all great people, but they don't really understand boundaries. Being the oldest grand-daughter, I've always been the babysitter for everything that happened at family gatherings. It was why I took a nanny job when I first got to Boston. I figured that was the best skill I had. Little did I know that there was a lot more to me than just caretaking.

"I'm not babysitting on this trip, Mom."

"Why would you say that?" she asked, turning to look at me.

"Because that's what I'm always stuck doing. I never get to do anything fun like the boys." Anger is stringing through my chest as I relive memories.

"You've always been such a great person with kids. I know I wouldn't have survived without your help when Frank was born."

I try not to let this sort of comment burrow its way into me. My family, even though I love them, is great at charm and using words to persuade people. Compliments aren't used often, but when they are, they're for a distinct purpose.

"Right, but I drove across the country to be at my brother's wedding, not to take care of everyone else's kids."

"Let's not worry about that right now. Why don't you go look in your old closet for something to pack for the trip?"

"Spencer is probably sleeping."

My mother leans on the counter and stares at me. "He's a cute guy. He's super respectful as well. You know we don't get a lot of that around here."

I want to say that she could change that, seeing as how she's got five sons, but I know how much my father influences the boys.

"I'm glad he came with me. It made the drive go by faster."

"Anything important you need to tell me?" my mom asks, giving me a side eye like she's waiting for something juicy to come out of my mouth.

Shaking my head, I say, "No. He's going to be my date for the wedding, but that's about it."

My mom reaches over and covers my hand with hers. "You never know, Millie. He might just realize how amazing you are and stick around."

Tears prick at my eyes and I try to muster up a smile. That's the first time she's complimented me in years. I should prob-ably figure out what angle she's trying to play, but I'm basking in the comment a little longer.

"Good morning," Spencer says, coming into the kitchen. He's wearing striped pajama pants and a black t-shirt that hugs all the right places. I didn't realize how toned he was before. Not that I should ogle him. #eternalfriend

"Good morning, Spencer," my mom says, pulling out several plates. "We'll let you two eat now before the morning rush starts."

Spencer sits next to me and gives me a sleepy grin.

"How did you sleep?" I ask quietly.

"Great. Although, I should've probably used a stuffie or two to keep me company." He grins and I push his shoulder harder than I should've, and he almost falls off the stool.

"Sorry, sorry," I say. Way to go, Millie. Just injure the poor guy.

"Millie couldn't sleep without a stuffie growing up. That was always her request for birthdays or Christmas." My mother is beaming at us and I'm silently dying inside. That's exactly what I didn't need Spencer to know. I just hope she doesn't bring up the fact I didn't stop sucking my thumb until I was nine.

"They're comforting. I had two favorites growing up. One was a large moose that my father brought back from a work trip, and the other was a small teddy bear I've had since I was born." Spencer stabs his fork into a bite of eggs so noncha-lantly, he doesn't see how surprised I am at such a simple comment. Can the guy stop being so great? He makes it difficult not to fall for him.

We eat our food and clean up our dishes before the rest of the boys come charging into the kitchen.

"Looks like we beat the rush," Spencer says with a chuckle.

"You're right. I just need to get a few clothes out of my old closet for today, if that's okay," I say, feeling awkward going into my old room while he's occupying it. It's like an invasion of privacy now that my feelings are going full speed ahead even though I've attempted to use the breaks.

He waves me forward. "Go for it. Do you know what time we're leaving?"

We walk down the hallway, and I open the door to my old room.

"Dad will probably come in any minute and say we've got fifteen minutes or something like that."

Spencer sits on the edge of the bed and says, "Really?"

I nod, trying to pry open one drawer in the old dresser. I didn't think I'd left that much here when I went to Boston. Once I finally get it unstuck, I pull out a couple pairs of pants and see that they're a size bigger than what I've been wearing for the last year.

I throw a few things and an old sweatshirt into a bag, pulling out my toiletry set from my regular suitcase.

Spencer disappeared while I packed. Maybe he went to get changed in the bathroom.

Walking down the hall, I see my dad in the living room. "Are we coming back here after the camping trip? And how many days will we be gone?"

He shakes his head. "No. We'll head up to the hotels in Danton for the week. So just bring everything."

Spencer walks in from the backyard, dirt all over him.

"What happened?" I ask, glancing from him to Frank and Eric trailing him.

With a small smile, Spencer says, "They wanted me to check out their bunker. It was cool."

Another shot of attraction flows through me again. Not that I'd ever brought anyone home as a boyfriend, but that Spencer, a self-declared city boy, will indulge my younger two brothers is a big deal.

"Go get changed," my dad says. "We're leaving in nineteen

minutes. We've got to beat everyone else to the campsite so we can get the best spot."

Of course, that would be what my father says in front of Spencer. I dread this camping trip. The extended family is one way in their regular life, but camping brings the competitive out of them. I just hope Spencer doesn't go running for the hills when this day is over. My family has been relatively mild up to this point. I'm crossing my fingers that they're not just gearing up for an explosion of crazy this week.

21

MILLIE

Dinner at the Olsen house isn't something I should've forgotten about. My mom had an old VHS tape where she'd recorded a show called *Seven Brides for Seven Brothers.* I'll never forget when the woman, also named Millie, gets to the cabin and the guys start to grab and go at the food she made like they're wild animals. So it's fitting that we continue this little tradition while we're camping and just about everywhere else.

We can recreate that scene every time we eat. But not having been around it for a couple years, it's a shock to my system. There is only one small roll left and an itty-bitty scoop of taco meat. And Spencer is here to witness the cave dweller-like characteristics that make up our family.

"How was the drive, Amelia?" my dad asks as he takes a bite of his food. He'd worked late the night before and had been too busy this morning to drill me with questions.

"We made it here. I've got the gas receipts for the truck."

He waves me off and says, "We'll get to that later. We don't need to talk about money while we're camping."

Nature would be the perfect backdrop for this scene except

I'm the only person in our family who knows how to close my mouth when I chew. I might need to invest in some earplugs if I'm going to hang out here much longer.

Beau's little pickup pulls up to the campsite, and I honestly didn't realize he wasn't here yet. Maybe I was too mortified by my family's behavior already. And for once in his life, he walks around to the passenger side and opens it to reveal his soon-to-be wife. I thought I'd have at least one more day before I had to face her.

"Did you save me anything?"

My mom gets up from the table and walks over to the cooler. "Of course, Beau. Here's yours right here. And I've got a plate for Trina."

His plate is heaping with food and hers has half the amount of his.

"I only got a small scoop, Mom. Is there something else I can eat?" I ask.

She frowns at me. "I'm not making a separate meal."

Sighing, I say, "I didn't ask you to. I'm just saying, are there more vegetables or something?"

"Go look in the stash."

I can hear the family talking once I walk over to the truck.

"Where've you been, son?" my dad asks.

Beau says, "I went to pick up Trina. Do you think we can use the limo after the wedding?"

"For sure. That's why we bought it. I'll have Carl drive it."

I frown. My dad is going to let his eighteen-year-old son drive a limo with my newly married brother and sister-in-law? That doesn't seem safe, but then again, he won't be drinking and it won't be a far drive from the wedding to the hotel.

I grab an apple and walk back over to sit next to Spencer.

Beau says hello to the rest of the family and sits down at the other end of the table with Trina to his side. I keep my gaze on the crumbs in front of me, pretending it's a four-course meal, so I don't have to look at her.

"Hey Trina," my mom says. "How was the drive here?"

Trina turns up her nose as she looks at nature around her and says, "It was great, thank you, Sharla."

I guess it's good that she's being kind of pleasant?

"Hey Spencer," Beau says, "I want to introduce you to my fiancée, Trina. Trina, this is Spencer, the guy who got me through college."

Spencer wipes his mouth with a napkin like a normal human and smiles in their direction. "It's nice to meet you, but I assure you, I wouldn't have made it through without Beau."

Trina gives him a quick smile before she lifts her fork to scoop up some of the taco meat.

"And you remember Amelia, right Tri?" Beau says.

I close my eyes, wishing I could be anywhere but here. So many moments of humiliation flash before my eyes and I just need one of those time-changer daggers that they use in the *Prince of Persia* so I can go back a few minutes and hide before the two of them arrive.

Spencer reaches over and takes my hand under the table, squeezing a couple of times. I slow my breathing and open my eyes, forcing a smile as I nod in her direction.

Trina's expression is curious, and she nods. "Yes, I remember Amelia. I was surprised to learn you live in Boston."

I freeze, not sure what she means by that. Her tone isn't giving me vibes of good or bad conversation, so I just squeeze Spencer's hand tighter and say, "Yeah, I'm working and going to school out there."

She nods approvingly and goes back to examining her plate. Is she nervous?

I turn to Spencer and he gives me a reassuring smile. He's also somehow finished his food in the last few seconds. Oh, wait, I think he might've shared his portion with me.

"I'll be okay," I whisper, trying to scoop some of the meat back onto his plate.

He shakes his head and says, "I'm good. You keep that and I'll wait until dinner."

"What's the schedule for the coming days?" my mom asks Beau.

He grins and says, "First thing is getting everyone fitted for their wedding clothes. Trina has a block reserved at the place she bought her gown from. The women will go there and the guys will be down the road at the tux rental place."

Frank and Eric groan from across the table.

"Then we wanted everyone to get to know each other with a cocktail hour the next day. There will be other activities and then the bachelor and bachelorette parties, of course. I can't remember most of it, but Trina will keep us on schedule."

I hadn't thought about the bachelorette party. If Trina still has the same friends from high school, I'll have to pretend to be sick or something. There's no way I'm going to survive a night out with them.

"The resort we're at will have activities for the kids," Trina says, glancing over at my younger brothers. "And we'll be having some dancing lessons to get us ready for a big number I want to have at the reception."

I frown. That's the last thing I want to do, especially in front of Trina and her posse. I'd never been the best on my feet with rhythm, but maybe I'd survive this embarrassment and never come back to visit.

"That will be great. I'm so excited about this. All the aunts and uncles are coming this afternoon." My mom stands up and walks over to clean some dishes from earlier. "Nothing like a family event to pull the family together."

As if her words had summoned other members of the Olsen extended family, two trucks pull up, along with an old Excursion. Let the family humiliation begin.

22

SPENCER

I don't think I've ever seen Millie so tight and nervous. But from the overall demeanor from Beau's fiancée, I can tell she was a Mean Girl in high school.

What caused me to reach over and take Millie's hand during the re-introduction? I'm not sure, but I'm glad I did. I might not be the best at a real lovey-dovey relationship, but I can make sure she comes through this week as a normal human, soothing as much of the hurts as possible and shielding her from others. I might have to up the game on my metaphorical armor, because this family has a distinct sense of humor.

I help clean up lunch with Millie, which seems to be a natural role for her here. As we're scraping the seasonings off the cast-iron pans, three families flood the campsite and I can tell why they got this family campground and the four surrounding it.

"How are you doing?" I ask, glancing at Millie out of the corner of my eye.

"Better than I thought, to be honest. Thanks for your help back there."

"Any time."

"You don't have to help with the dishes all the time." Millie says it like she'd love to be doing anything else.

"Why don't you take a break and I'll finish up here?"

She shakes her head. "No, I'm good. You're the guest."

"I'm also your date for this wedding."

Millie pauses and turns to me, trying to move a chunk of hair away from her eye with her forearm since her hands are wet. "The wedding isn't for several days."

"So? If I were you, I'd need an armed guard to surround me with all the drama coming your way."

She chuckles. "Now you can understand why I was reluctant to come."

Nodding, I say, "Yeah, that's the hard thing. I think your parents take advantage of you."

"I know, but it's all part of being an obedient daughter, you know? I don't know how to break out of that role."

"I have zero advice, but I think saying no every once in a while might help."

She nods but says nothing as she continues to scrub at the pan. It looks a lot cleaner than the one I'm working on. She dries it and cleans the camp stove, applying water to the first section and then oil to finish it. I'm amazed at how she knows how to do all this, but I guess if it's something she's grown up doing, it would be easy.

Sharla comes over. "Oh, thank you, Spencer, for helping with the dishes." She turns to the other adults and I can't believe that she completely overlooked her daughter.

"Millie did most of it."

Sharla turns back to me and says, "Sorry, what?"

"I'm not good at this. Millie is the one who got everything cleaned up so well."

After several eye blinks, I say, "Millie deserves a thank you."

Sharla smiles and says, "She knows that I'm grateful."

Millie's eyes are wide with confusion, and I debate whether I should be in this kind of debate.

"She'd probably like to hear it."

After a long breath, Sharla says, "Thank you, Millie. It does look nice." Not the most genuine compliment, but it's got to be better than what Millie has dealt with her entire life.

"Thank you." Millie touches my arm gently and then goes back to putting away the pans in the large tote they came out of.

I'm bombarded with introductions of all the aunts and uncles as their children wreak havoc on the campground before disappearing into the woods and over to the small river next to it.

One woman, who I think is named Tonya, looks at Millie and says, "Will you keep an eye on the little ones, Millikins?"

I hold my breath, trying to will her to speak her mind. She looks at me and hesitates, as if still debating what to do. And then she nods and walks over to the creek.

I chase after her and say, "What happened back there?"

Millie is wringing her hands together as she lengthens her stride. "I don't know what's worse, taking care of their kids or having them badger me with questions and requests for money."

Frowning, I say, "Your aunts and uncles ask you for money?"

She blows out a breath and nods. "They think that I'm making bank in Boston. I haven't told my parents I'm no longer nannying full time."

"And your parents are okay with them asking this?" I must've grown up in what looks like movie conditions compared to this.

"They don't say much, just treating it like a joke."

"I feel bad that I even encouraged you to come." We sit on a couple of bigger rocks near the water and she scans left to right. I can see her lips moving as she counts the active bodies over here. Danny, Eric, and Frank are in the middle of the river, the three of them dripping as they push each other into the water.

She shrugs. "It's not the worst thing in the world, but I always doubt myself when I come back, like my time in Boston has been for nothing. Or that it was all a dream. I just wish I could stand up to them."

"Let's practice." I'm pushing a lot, but this woman in front of me can't seem to see how amazing she is. I just want her to use the spunk inside of her this week. It's there, it's just a sleeping dragon ever since we drove over the Colorado state line.

"Practice?" she says, scrunching her nose at the thought.

"Yeah, when I was working on my acting, I would practice my lines at least thirty to forty times before the take. By the time it came to say them, I could do it without hesitation. Maybe if you practice this, you won't panic when you can say no."

Millie glances out at the water and bites her bottom lip, drawing my attention there. This beautiful human, who's been through so much, makes me want to tell her how important she is, how incredible she is for all that she does. But I worry she won't believe it right now.

I make my voice go higher, trying to imitate her aunt and say, "Millikins, will you watch my kids for the next week?"

She turns to me, laughing loudly, and shakes her head.

"Please, I just need to relax and we're at a wedding for someone else's son, so I should totally get a break," I continue.

"Stop," she says, trying to catch her breath again.

"What do you say, Millikins?"

"No."

"Good. What was that again?" I say in my normal voice.

"No, I won't watch your kids for the entire week."

I press my hand against my chest in mock shock and say, "How dare you say something like that? You will watch my kids while I catch up with the rest of the family."

Millie's smile fades, and she stares at her hand in her lap.

I reach over and touch her shoulder, trying to move so I can see into her eyes. "I was just trying to help you, Millie. I'm sorry."

"You're fine. It's just something I need to work through."

There's a splash of water and our attention turns to the river. Small arms and legs pop up to the surface before they disappear below the water.

Millie is up in seconds and runs to the water before diving in to swim through it.

She lifts the toddler out of the water and over to dry land. Before I can even make it to her, she's got the toddler over her leg and is pounding his back at a downward angle. Water comes out of his mouth and then he cries.

There's a look of determination on her face. She gives the little guy a hug before carrying him over to where all the adults are sitting.

"I'm off duty," Millie says, before handing over the soaking child to his mom and walking straight for a path in the woods.

It might not have been a firm no, but that was more progress than I'd expected from her in such a short time. Now I just need to make sure she's okay.

23

MILLIE

I can't believe I did that. First off, I should've been paying attention to the kids instead of practicing saying no with Spencer. But it felt good to drop off Sonny and walk away. Powerful, even.

I walk through a path that crosses over the river and I lean on the bridge railing, focusing on the water below. It's always had a calming effect for me.

"Hey," Spencer says, standing next to me. "You delivered that perfectly."

"Then why do I feel awful?" I ask, turning to look at him. And then I have to turn my gaze away because if I look at him too long, I might do something dumb. Like lean over and press my lips to his. But since I've never actually kissed anyone, I'll probably bungle it up. Where do I put my hands and how long? Never mind. I don't need Spencer to forever be weird around me. It's best to rein in my emotions.

Spencer is quiet for several moments and then says, "Well, if you've toed the line for your entire life, it's probably scary to go against what people think of you or what they perceive your worth is."

"I should've been paying attention the whole time."

"No, you shouldn't be forced to watch other people's kids all the time just because you're the only girl in your family."

I nod, my mind understanding that, but my heart still feels like I screwed up royally.

"So what do I do now?" I ask. "Am I supposed to go sit in their little circle and listen to their stories about trying every pain medication on the market?"

Spencer chuckles, but it fades out when he can see I'm being serious. "You do what you want. Stay respectful, but set the boundaries you need to keep you sane."

"You make it sound so easy," I say, picturing telling my parents anything that goes against what their family has been doing for generations.

"It will probably take practice. I remember when I was young, my parents had to tell their parents that we wouldn't be attending family functions on the day of Christmas anymore."

I turn, curious about where this is going. Spencer is using his hands to describe everything, and there's another prick of attraction setting in. I think it's getting stronger, and I'm not sure how to tamp it down. Maybe some forced time apart would help. But he's my lifeline right now. I don't know if I would've survived any part of the trip without him. Well, seeing my brothers is refreshing.

"I remember my mom crying for a long time because her parents were super disappointed. But my dad was there and held her, trying to comfort her. The first two years were hard, but after that, we started traveling for Christmas and making it about our own little family. It's hard and scary to do things that go against other people's expectations, but would you rather have this dread every time you come to visit your parents? Or would you like to come here and feel you don't have the obligations they've always given you?"

With a quick laugh, I lift my hand to brush at a tear. "Obviously the other one."

"Then you've got to stand up now, so you can set those boundaries and enjoy life. You won't dread coming here to see your family. What have they done for a babysitter while you were away in Boston?"

His question has me thinking. What do they do when I'm not here to conveniently parent for them?

Without hesitation, I lean over and wrap my arms around Spencer's waist. He wraps me up in his arms, and I don't think I've ever felt this comfortable. Except at the hotel a few days ago.

"How do you know so much about life?" I ask, my voice somewhat muffled by his shirt.

"I might've had a different childhood, but my parents didn't shelter me from these kinds of experiences."

I mull that over and squeeze tighter. "Thank you."

Spencer lets go and I feel the coolness away from his body heat. "I need a drink. Do you want to come back with me?"

I stare through the trees, picturing my aunts and uncles and parents all circled up in their fold up chairs. "Give me a few minutes. I'll be there soon."

Spencer disappears and I go back to gazing out over the water, feeling some of the tension go out of me.

I'm not sure how long I'm there until I hear a broken twig and jump, turning to see Trina walking carefully across the bridge. Why didn't I just go with Spencer? I don't need any solo confrontations right now.

It isn't until she's only a few feet away from me when she looks up to see me standing there.

"Trying to escape too?" she asks.

I'm too stunned to answer right off, but finally say, "Yeah. That's kind of my whole life."

Trina stands next to me and I hold my breath. Is she going

to push me into the water below? Put gum in the back of my hair so I have to cut it all off again?

"Look, I know we haven't always been good friends–"

I snort, which is quite daring of me considering the woman standing next to me. It cuts off her words though, and she says, "What?"

It takes everything in me, but I think "What would Spencer do?"

"I don't think we were even in the realm of friends, Trina."

She frowns. "You're right. Beau was hoping I'd ask you to be my bridesmaid."

I'm speechless. It doesn't matter how many dreams or nightmares I've had since high school ended, the resulting scenario never included her in my post-high school life.

"Um, can you say that again? I didn't quite catch it."

Trina gives a high-pitched laugh and says, "I bet you didn't. Do you want to be a bridesmaid?"

From the look on her face, it's not a convincing sentiment. "You said Beau wants you to ask me, but do you actually want me in the bridal party?"

She blinks her fake lashes as if I said that in another language. "What do you mean? All I need is a yes or no."

My brain debates her words for a few moments and the conversation I'd just had with Spencer moments before comes up. "No."

Trina's lips pinch together. "You're turning down the chance to be a bridesmaid?"

"I'm here to support my brother. I don't want a pity invite."

"Kudos to you for sticking to your guns." Trina's eyes narrow in on my face.

We stand there, silent for several moments. I'm not sure what to do, so of course my body brushes past fight and flight and heads straight for the freeze setting.

"I'm sorry for what I did before. For all those years of

torture." Trina's words are soft, and I can hear the sincerity in them.

I feel like I've just had an icy bucket of water dumped over me. "What?"

She lets out a long breath and says, "I never should've done any of that to you. I, well, I, uh, don't expect you to forgive me. Just know that I am sorry. For everything."

Everything about her expression seems sincere, but I've been duped into things before.

"Thank you for saying that." I pull my upper lip between my teeth. My high school bully is saying sorry? This has to be another timeline I've stumbled into.

"Is there anything I can do to make things right? Do you need me to pay for therapy?"

I'm not sure what to say to that. There's been plenty of crazy in my life, but I've been able to manage through talking to my roommates, and especially Spencer.

"I appreciate the offer, but I'm only here for the wedding, and then I'll head back to Boston."

We're quiet for a moment before she says, "That's really cool you work out there. What's your job?"

Where do I start for this? We might be on the acquaintance level now, instead of enemies, but I'm still leery that this will change and quickly. "I started as a nanny but quit a few months ago and began going to college online. I do little things here and there for work, mostly to pay the bills, but I'm just trying to finish up my school stuff before I look for a full-time job."

And then I turn to see Trina nearly in tears.

"Um, are you okay? Was it something I said?"

"That's great that you've been able to figure out what you want for your life. I've just never been able to do anything without my parents instructing me to do it."

Confused, I say, "What about Beau? I can't think they'd be super excited that you're marrying him."

She uses her finger to dab gently beneath her eyes. "Yeah, he isn't even on their list of top ten guys to marry. But I put my foot down. As quirky as he is, I love Beau. I'm excited to marry him."

"Is that why you're getting married so soon?"

She nods and says, "I didn't want to chance having my parents ruin the wedding or push it off even further."

More tears cascade down her cheeks and I'm not prepared for this moment. Before, I was the one to cry because of something she did to me. But this is the most real I've ever seen her. I pat her back gently, unsure of how to proceed here.

"Thank you," is all I can say. I turn to look at the river again, trying to figure out what to do now. This was not on my bingo card for this trip.

Trina pulls back, wiping away at the tears. "A few minutes ago I said that Beau wanted me to ask you to be in the wedding with us. But I would love to have you with me. You'd probably be a better fit as maid of honor than my sister."

"What do you mean?"

"Elaine used to be my best friend, but she's been acting weird ever since Beau proposed. I don't know if she's just trying to side with my parents because they're not happy or what."

She glances at me and then says, "I really screwed this whole thing up, didn't I? I had planned to say I was sorry and then ask you to be a bridesmaid." How did the girl I remember from high school turn into a normal woman with feelings?

My body involuntarily coughs, and I do a quick scan of the surrounding areas. I'm being pranked. I have to be.

The only pranks that should be pulled are the ones Evie and Owen do when decorating our front yard.

"You want me–Amelia Olsen–to be a bridesmaid? I figured the world would be burning before that happened."

She glances down at her fingers and says, "Well, the group I hung out with in high school stopped hanging out with me once I was admitted to rehab for alcohol."

Oh. I didn't see that coming.

"I hope that you'll help me through the next week. Mostly I need someone on my side against my mother, who has been trying to relive the wedding she never got. They got married at the courthouse because she was pregnant with me."

The gossip just keeps coming. I'm standing next to her like a wooden statue, unsure of how to react. I never thought I'd see the human side of Trina Burkhead.

She glances up at me and I say, "Sure, I can do that. I'm not sure what that entails, though."

And in a move that my imagination would never have conjured before this moment, she leans over and pulls me into a tight hug. "Thank you, thank you. That will be perfect. We'll get your gown picked out tomorrow and then you can help me figure out what to do for my bachelorette party."

I don't want to mention that if she's asking me to be in her bridal party, she might be scraping the bottom of the barrel, but I decide to keep my mouth shut for that one. By the time we walk back to the campsite, I'm exhausted from the rollercoaster of emotions I've gone through in just the past hour.

But there's some light for me being here. Some healing and closure for all I'd been through at Trina's hand and some level of empathy for what she's been through.

I wait for that gut wrenching feeling I get when things aren't right. But all I can feel is that telling Trina yes is the right thing to do. Maybe this won't be the worst trip ever.

24

SPENCER

I've been sitting at a table behind the group of adults as they chatter away about their lives, but my mind is still over by the brook, hoping Millie is okay. I'm ready to go look for her again, feeling a lot more like a mother hen than a twenty-six-year-old man should, but she comes through the trees moments later. And she looks... happy.

That's something I wasn't expecting.

She slides onto the bench next to me with a grin and says, "I did it."

"Did what?" I ask, trying to figure out why she's whispering.

"I said no."

I turn to her, grinning. "That's great. Why did you have to say it and to whom?"

Millie glances around and then leans closer to me. She's still wet from the dip in the river and I can see goosebumps all along her skin.

"You're freezing. I'll go get your stuff so you can change."

She puts her hand on my forearm. I pause, looking at her.

"I said no to being a bridesmaid."

Just then, I glance up and see Trina coming from the same

direction as the bridge. I didn't think it was possible for someone to scowl so deeply.

"She asked you to be a bridesmaid and you said no?" When Millie nods, I laugh and say, "Congrats on that one, but can we get you warm? I don't know the way to the hospital from here."

Millie chuckles. "She then asked me again, and I said yes."

I frown. "Wait, what?"

She tells me about the conversation she'd had with her future sister-in-law and while I'm kind of sad I missed it, from the look on Millie's face, she needed this.

"I'll grab my stuff and change. That wind is making me cold." She gets up, looking like she's walking on clouds.

Beau walks over and says, "Have you seen Millie?"

I point toward the truck and say, "She's going to change. Why?"

This is the most nervous I've ever seen Beau. Usually he plays everything off like that was his main plan.

"I'm waiting to hear how it goes with Trina. There is a lot of water under the bridge between those two. I just want to make sure that everything's good between the two of them." And that's the most heartfelt thing I've heard him say. Ever.

A few moments later, I can see Millie walking back toward us.

Trina sidles up next to Beau and says, "Millie has accepted the role of bridesmaid."

Beau grins. "That's awesome. I'm glad you'll be up there with us, Millikins."

The adult circle overhears, and they all smile and nod, like they totally expected this. Part of me feels like I'm in a movie where I have to suspect everyone of betraying the innocent girl. But Millie obviously believes Trina. I just hope Trina didn't do it to further the tirade from high school. And if Beau is a part of it, this will be the last time I ever speak with him.

I have so many questions, but I don't want to ask them in front of the bride and groom.

We play a few games of cards, and the older adults get up to prepare dinner. Some aunts and uncles have even gone to search for their kids periodically, which I point out to Millie with a nudge. At least she can breathe easier that she didn't do something unforgivable.

"Millie, will you come help us with dinner?" one of the aunts asks.

I make eye contact with Sharla and give a little shake of the head. I don't know if she completely understands what I mean by that, but she looks at Millie and then back at the aunts.

"I think Millie needs a break. She's not here very often."

"We need to discuss some wedding things anyway," Trina says, reaching over the table and holding Millie's hand for a moment. I expect to feel that suspicious strain that has been going through me ever since Beau arrived with Trina, but it seems like this is all real.

When I turn to see Millie's face, she's near to tears.

"Are you okay?" I whisper, trying not to draw any attention to her.

She nods and sniffles. "Yes, thanks."

Beau deals out some cards, adding a hand for Frank and Eric, who slide next to us at the table. They're covered in dirt and something green, but I can't tell what it is.

"What do you have planned for the bachelor party?" Beau asks as he deals out the cards.

"Do we get to go to that?" Frank asks, playing one of his cards on the discard pile.

Beau shakes his head. "Probably not, Frankie."

I open my mouth to respond and realize I have nothing. Being the planner of the bachelor party hasn't hit my brain to-do list yet.

"That's a great question. I'll have to think about that." I scan the scenery for anything that might spark an idea. "What about doing something with a campfire?"

Beau turns up his nose and says, "We're doing that right now. Let's do something else."

"How many people are you planning to invite?" I ask, knowing I'll have to research this the minute we get back to a cell service area.

"At least the five groomsmen."

I nod, wishing we'd stayed in a hotel room right now. Sure, things are a little strained with Beau because of the break of our companies, but I want to be a good friend to him and make sure it is worthwhile.

"What if we combine the bachelor and bachelorette parties and go to the drive-in movie?" Millie asks.

Trina claps her hands together. "I love that idea."

Beau nods. "Yeah, that would work. Maybe we can have dinner before it."

"Ruby's Diner?" I ask, remembering that Millie had mentioned missing their food.

Millie grins and says, "That would be great. Then we can bring some snacks for the movie." She turns to Beau and asks, "Do Mom and Dad still have the giant bean bags?"

He nods. "We could take the shell off the big truck you all brought and use that to seat more people. I think my old boombox still works for the sound too."

For the first time since I'd been with the Olsens, there might be hope for this family. They have some strange ideas on a lot of things, but they're willing to compromise, which I wouldn't have imagined when we arrived yesterday. Proof that not all first impressions are correct.

Millie has definitely surprised me. I hope she keeps doing that for the foreseeable future.

I need her in my life.

25

MILLIE

We're in the Twilight Zone. We have to be. Because my brother getting excited about doing a joint bachelor and bachelorette party at the drive-in must be some weird wrinkle in time.

It's that, or he loves Trina. Which I didn't think could happen.

We've set up our tents and eaten dinner, which no one asked me to clean up for once. I can breathe without the anxiety squeezing my lungs to death.

I meet up with Spencer after brushing my teeth in the bathroom. He takes my hand in his and squeezes. "How are you doing?"

I nod. "I'm cautiously hopeful."

I can barely see his eyebrows cinch together under the headlight he's wearing and I have to laugh at the seriousness of it.

"I'm surprised by all that's happened today, but it feels good. Like all the parts that were broken are slowly coming together. Thanks to you."

Shaking his head, he says, "No, you did that on your own. I just gave you a gentle push. Be careful and let me know if you need help with anything this week."

I don't want this conversation to end. "What about you? Have you checked into that dating app?" I ask with a small smile. Half of me is hoping he has so I can avoid heartbreak later, while the other part wants him to see me as a potential dating candidate.

Spencer smiles and says, "No. I'll be fine without it."

Frowning, I say, "You're the one who keeps telling me to take the leap. To push through my fears or practice." I try to look him in the eyes, but he glances down, examining the palm of his hand. "Spencer, if Scotty Duncan were here, what would you say to him?"

"I'm not going there. Not right now." His voice sounds strangled and for the first time since I've known him, he looks vulnerable and like he might crumble into a million pieces. He lets go of my hand and backs up. I thought my terror at telling my family no was a big deal, but this might be even harder for him. I just need to figure out how to help. Maybe somehow acting like our conversation is for my benefit might help him open back up.

"You've taught me to stand up for me. I'll leave it alone for now, but I want to help you like you've helped me." I change the subject. "What about conversational topics when dating or with new people? Help me with those."

It's like he transforms back into his confident self when I ask him that. "I think the next thing would be deeper conversation."

"Okay," I say, a little nervous about how that sounds. "What do you mean by that?"

"When you first meet people, you go through all the surface-level questions. What do they do for work and their free time? Do they like to travel or have any allergies?"

I laugh. "You talk to women about allergies?"

Spencer nods. "One time I went on a date with this woman and she ordered something that had almonds in it. Her face swelled up like a balloon and I had to jab her with an EpiPen. I've never forgotten that one and now that is a standard question in the rotation."

I try to picture Spencer's reaction to the whole thing. Then I turn my attention to his statement. Deeper conversation.

We'd practiced earlier, and it had worked with me saying no to my aunts. Why not practice now with someone I'm genuinely curious about?

"Did you have to worry about your image a lot when you were acting?"

Spencer's jaw tightens and the movement of the vein tells me that this conversation went a lot deeper and faster than he expected.

"Being on camera is hard as it is. There's so much to remember, like the lines and where to stand. How to interact with the other characters in the scene. Those are long days and as a growing boy, I fluctuated as I grew. I got negative comments about me getting chunky and then again, when I'd gotten taller, that I needed to eat a hamburger."

"I think you're handsome anyway," I say, wishing I could rein the words back in after I'd said them.

"Oh, yeah? Thank you for that. What about Juan?" he asks, giving me a lopsided grin.

Shaking my head, I say, "I don't know a Juan."

"The guy you've been crushing on for years?"

My mind is cloudy as I finally remember Jordan. The mythical guy I'd always compared everyone to. But sitting here, next to Spencer, it's a simple decision. I've basically traded out Jordan for Spencer in my brain.

"What about Jordan?" I ask.

"What are some things you'd want to ask him?" His lips

turn down for a moment before he gives me a warm smile. Is he jealous? Or am I just hoping he is?

"How about I practice with you a bit more?" I ask.

Spencer nods. "Find some topic they love to do or talk about. If he loves sports, learn a couple of terms or phrases and that can get you into a position where you can ask more questions. People love feeling helpful. So for you, I'll ask you when was the last time you thought about taking pictures?"

I put my toiletry bag down on the table at our campsite and take a seat on the bench next to it. "To be honest, it's been a while. Probably the fight-or-flight situation of adulthood. Will I have enough money to pay X bill? Survival mode is where I'm at right now."

"I keep thinking about the photos in your room. You've got a good eye for that. Making something that I usually think is boring look interesting."

"I think it's like graphic design. I worry about putting too much pressure on myself and then burning out. Just because I'm good at something doesn't mean I want to put a price on it and try to sell it to the highest bidder."

Spencer's mouth opens and then closes. He stares at me for several moments before saying, "I guess I've never thought of it like that. There's always the saying that you should do what you love."

"Or do what you kind of love and then save the thing you absolutely love for when you need a break from your actual job." It's something I came up with during my first semester in college a few months ago. It's why I changed my major from graphic design to business. I like the idea of learning how to run a profitable business and maybe help others while keeping my stuff for myself.

"I don't know who's the better coach," he says with a grin.

Am I still in the "sister" category? Or is there a chance he could like me?

Either way, I'm probably heading for a heartbreak because my emotional train is full speed ahead.

26

SPENCER

I'm not the best camper. There's no way I'm saying that in front of Beau's dad and family, but it's the truth. The adults sat around the campfire for hours and I got so bored I wasn't sure what to do. Millie and I went for a walk over by the bridge at sunset, and it was nice to get away and spend some more time with her. I don't know if I'm breaking any bro codes by the feelings I'm having when Millie is around, but I won't worry about that right now. Beau is distracted enough with this wedding.

These feelings are probably because we've been together almost non-stop in the past several days. And I'm protective of her since her family is crazy. Once we get back to Boston, we'll go back to hanging out like normal, and it won't be a big deal.

And her thoughts on what to do for work. I wonder if that's a defense mechanism or something she actually believes will help her career. Either way, I'll support her.

I wake up this morning to a deflated air mattress with Beau and a couple of his brothers snoring loudly next to me. The temptation to throw something at them because they're getting sleep and I'm not is high.

Instead, I shiver when I get out of my sleeping bag to find my clothes. Or the clothes that Beau lent me. I have to suck in to get the button to go through the hole and the shirts feel like they're plastered to my body. Just a few more hours, I tell myself. Then I can wear my regular clothes that fit well and don't remind me of the comments people made when I was chunkier.

Sharla is the only one I can see once I step out of the tent. She's flipping pancakes and then putting bacon on the grill.

"Do you need help with this?" I ask, rubbing my eyes as I walk over.

"Oh Spencer," she says, smiling at me. "I'm surprised you're up this early. Go back to sleep."

"I'm good. The boys are snoring loudly and you shouldn't be the only one out here cooking for everyone."

Sharla's smile disappears and she says, "That's just my role in the family, son. I make sure everyone is full."

"Doesn't that get old?" I ask, taking the whisk from her and stirring together what looks to be a batch of pancake mix.

"There are times I wish it wasn't like this. But I've been doing this for almost thirty years now. Everything would fall apart if I didn't do this."

"It's okay to enlist help from your family. And not just the female ones," I say, slowing down my stirring as some of the flour jumps out.

"John would never allow that. He thinks a woman's place is in the kitchen."

I grit my teeth. What is it with this family and their disregard for people's needs? As well as the lack of communication.

"It's worth a conversation."

She nods, going back to flipping the pancakes onto a large platter. "Is that why Millie didn't want to come home?" she asks, with tears in her eyes.

"If all she's ever done is babysit when she comes back, it

would be hard to feel a part of the family. And when you thank me and not her for helping, it's not good. I know I'm not your family, but being taken for granted isn't something I'd want for my life. Everyone expects you to be the one to make the meals, just like they expect Millie to babysit. Something needs to change."

A tear drips down Sharla's cheek, and I'm not sure what to do about it.

"I didn't mean to make you cry," I say, reaching over to give her a side hug.

"You're good, Spencer. You're a wonderful boy. Thank you for talking to me about this."

We work in silence for a while longer, and then the tents open as people wake up. Millie sits next to me with a sleepy smile when we finish cooking the food.

After everyone has finished eating, Sharla tells her boys and her husband that they're on clean-up duty. There's a lot of staring and a hushed argument between husband and wife, but whatever she ends up saying to him has him telling the boys to help with cleanup, while he stalks off to his truck and drives off.

"What happened there?" Millie asks in awe.

I shrug. "I'm not sure. Maybe she got sick of doing everything and said no."

Millie turns to me with wide eyes. "You did that?"

I shake my head. "No, that was all your mom."

"You're rubbing off on all of us, Spencer," Millie says, laughing a bit.

"You might be rubbing off on me too," I say. It's not something I should admit or say because then things get sticky.

The overall feeling between us the past few days is that we've been closer, but I don't want to lead her on when I know I might not be the best option as a significant other in her life, should she even want that. Millie seems like a woman who would stick with something once her mind is made up, but she's already got her heart set on this Jackson guy.

She means the world to me, and if he's the guy she wants, I need to respect it. It will hurt like hell, but I'll protect her the best way I can.

27

MILLIE

We made it through the camping trip and I'm a bit on edge from what's coming. Maybe it was a rash decision to agree to be a bridesmaid. I keep thinking this is all some elaborate prank, but if Beau is in on it, I'll be crushed. Thinking about how I haven't even cracked open my computer since leaving Boston only adds to my nerves.

Spencer seems off too, like he's not his usual excited self, but then again, that could be a camping hangover. Sleeping on a mattress doesn't make for the best mood.

Beau drives us up to Danton in the big truck, Trina in the passenger side and me sitting next to Spencer with my other four brothers filling in the seats. It's loud and there's plenty of laughter and bickering. My parents made it seem like this would be a mini vacation from their kids.

We check into the hotel and I'm sort of disappointed there isn't a shortage of rooms, like on our trip to Bitter Springs. I could use a good cuddle with Spencer. Strike that thought and stop thinking about how good he smells. I've never been good at knowing what cologne goes with which scent, but whatever he uses, I'm a fan.

I'm assigned to be in a suite with my family and I'm wishing I could be in a smaller room with one of my female cousins.

Not having a vehicle to drive and being stuck in a hotel room with my parents makes me think of all the trips we took as a family before I flew the nest. And has me wishing for my bed back in Boston. Am I fourteen again?

"All the ladies are meeting in the lobby to head to the dress fitting," my mom says after checking her phone.

I'd almost forgotten about this part. Hopefully, this store isn't one of those that only have sizes below a ten. I'm not fat, but I'm not stick thin either, and I don't want to worry about not fitting into something Trina chose.

A text comes through on my phone.

Hillary: How's it going? I've got a whole post ready to send you for revenge, if needed.

Me: Thanks for the offer, but I think I'll be okay. She asked me to be a bridesmaid.

Hillary: No! Really? So now you have to wear an ugly dress?

I laugh out loud as we head down the elevator.

"What's so funny?" my mom asks, trying to lean over and see what I'm looking at.

I turn off my phone and tuck it into a pocket, smiling to myself. Maybe I've misjudged Hillary all along. She's not really terrifying so much as she is sarcastic.

My mom drives me and my two aunts over to the dress shop and it's a nice, big building, something Bitter Springs wouldn't be able to support.

"How can I help you?" the woman behind the counter asks.

"We're here to try on dresses for the Burkhead-Olsen wedding," my mother says, giving the woman a smile.

The woman pinches her lips together and nods, typing away at the keyboard. "I don't know if I have you in here."

"Trina Burkhead?" I say, trying to get going on this. I've

been subjected to a lot of embarrassment in my life, but I don't want to have that happen to my whole extended family. Yes, we're dysfunctional, but I'll still defend them from haters.

"Ah, I think I found you. Your appointment isn't for another two hours."

I frown, not happy about that. I don't really want to walk around town for that long.

There's a section of the wall where I can see a familiar figure. Trina is standing on one of the big platforms, with someone fluffing the dress behind her.

Why would she be here and we aren't supposed to be here for another two hours? Was it something with the tailoring?

A spark of irritation hits me.

"Let's go get something to eat," one of my aunts says.

Instead, I walk straight forward, needing some kind of explanation. I'm done playing games.

"You look amazing," I say as I walk through the open doorway and toward Trina. The dress she's wearing is flattering in all the right spots and fits her so well, it could've been made for her.

Trina turns to me, all smiles. "Isn't it great? I didn't think I'd find the dress that I'd say yes to, but with the flower decor and the princess ballgown look, it's perfect."

The upper section has a cap-sleeve on one side that slopes down under her other arm. The beading is small and intricate, but it's beautiful.

"Where's the rest of your family? I've got a bunch of options picked out for them to try on." Trina looks past me, searching for the others.

"The lady up front told us our appointment wasn't for another two hours, but I saw you here and wondered if that was a mistake."

Trina shook her head. "No, this is when I booked for everyone. My mom is trying on a dress, along with my sister and other family members. Tell them to come in."

I'm trying to figure out what to believe here. Of course, my suspicions are high because of our shared past, but I have to believe that people can change, right?

A woman with similar features to Trina walks out in a rose-colored dress that looks similar to the prom dresses in the late nineties. Hillary wasn't kidding about the ugly dress.

Older Trina clone glances at me and then up at Trina. "Who's this?"

"This is Beau's sister. Millie, this is my mom, Daphne."

"It's nice to meet you," I say with a bob of my head.

"What are you doing here so early?"

I'm surprised by her brisk tone and it takes a couple of extra seconds to figure out a response. "Trina told us to come now."

Daphne glances up at her daughter and says, "I'm sorry, dear. The boutique said they needed to move Beau's family until later to accommodate everyone."

Trina's mouth turns into a thin line. "There's room. They can start now."

I know she said something earlier about her having a hard time going against her parents, but she's standing strong on what she wants right now. This is a tougher scenario than when I took Sonny back to my aunt at the campground, but this helps me see why I need to voice my opinions. I'll file this under "Things I Never Thought I'd Learn from Trina."

Daphne scowls. "There just isn't enough room. Didn't you say they would be bringing at least ten people? That's over-whelming to the staff here."

"You're almost done, mother, and so is Elaine. Your sisters already finished picking their dresses. We'll let the Olsens start looking for the styles they want to try on so we don't have to be here all day."

As controlling as it seems Trina's mother is, I can agree with

Trina that I don't want to be here for several hours. Even sixty minutes might be too long in a place like this.

If she'd had the time, it would've been cool to see what Evie could come up with for an event like this. She used to work in a wedding dress shop in Boston and she has skills to put anything together. I can mend clothes, but that's about it.

Trina turns to me and says, "Go tell them to come back and we'll show them some ideas I had."

Mrs. Burkhead's shock turns to fury, but I walk over to the door and wave for the group to come in.

"Trina says we can come check out some dresses while we wait for a dressing room to open up." I want to tell them all to be quiet and to act normally, since it seems they're determined to talk over one another. That's not a good look for the higher society people.

Trina is no longer on the podium, but her mother is, sneering down at everyone. It's not until my mother looks up at her that her face changes, as if she's putting on a mask.

"Hello Sharla," she says, blinking her eyes rapidly. She looks like she's trying to fly away with just her eyelashes.

"Daphne. I didn't realize you were Trina's mother, but now I see the resemblance."

"Did you not do a parent dinner or meeting?" I ask quietly.

"We haven't had time," Daphne says. "This has all been such a whirlwind romance."

My mother's jaw is stiffer than I've ever seen her, and I can tell there's history there.

Trina comes out of the dressing room and greets everyone. "All right ladies, I'm hoping to get you all outfitted today so they'll have time for any last-minute adjustments for the wedding. My colors are rose and sage, like these," she says, pointing to two different dresses on the wall.

"If you'll walk around and look for a dress in those colors that you want to try on, we'll get going on it."

"Do you know Daphne, Mom?" I whisper next to her.

My mom tries to give me a smile while saying through her teeth, "We were best friends in high school. We had a falling out because your dad chose me to be his date to the winter formal."

"How did I not know this?" Maybe that was a lot of the reason the Burkheads had it out for the Olsens. And now Beau marrying into the family was healing it in some way? Then again, I can't see him healing anything normally.

"It was in the past. We've moved on."

It doesn't look like Daphne agrees with that.

I search the shop for something that would be comfortable and in my size. Sure, I might've gone down a size in jeans when I moved to Boston, but I will never be on a runway.

There are two dresses I pull from the rack, one in each color. I walk over to the sitting area and wait for a dressing room to open. It's then that I see Daphne walk out in a lacy white dress.

She's grinning and looking at her reflection in the mirror, as if this is the dress she would wear to her own wedding. Thirty years ago.

"Why are you trying on wedding dresses?" I ask, trying to keep my tone neutral. There are others in this area, but they're bustling about, not paying attention to anyone else.

"It's just the thrill of the look," Daphne says, still admiring her image in the mirror. Trina comes through the curtains with my mother, helping her carry several dresses as they look for a room.

Daphne ducks behind her and into the changing room. That's weird.

"This one is open, Millie," Trina says, pointing to a dressing room.

I nod and take the dresses inside, avoiding the look in the

mirror as I undress. Not that I'm ashamed of my body, it's just weird to stare at it when I'm in a bra and underwear.

I slip on the rose-colored dress but don't zip it up because it hugs all the wrong spots in my midsection, and it clashes more than ever with my hair. That might be a good thing to add to the regret of asking me to be included in the wedding party, but if I'm going to get a nice dress, I want to feel good in it.

The sage-colored one is heavy and while it's okay in shape, it's not something I'll be wanting to wear for hours on end. I wish I'd pulled a few other dresses to try on so I didn't have to get dressed again to go search.

"How's it going in there, Millie?" Mom asks.

"Not good," I blurt. This honesty thing Spencer has me focused on is taking over.

"Can I see one of them?"

At least I hadn't taken off the sage dress all the way. I slide my arms through the holes and reach back to hold the two sides together without zipping it up.

"That looks great," Mom says with a smile. Then she glances up at my face and her smile falters. "You don't like it."

"It feels like I'd be carrying a weight vest around. Having to wear it all day is not ideal."

"Okay, let me zip you up, and we'll go in search of something else." I let Mom do just that and shuffle out in my sock-covered feet to search for more dresses.

There are several more voices now and I turn to see a few women who look familiar. Maybe they were a year or two older than us in high school? One is pregnant, but they all look exactly like they did five years ago. I try to hide behind a rack of dresses, but don't make it in time.

"Is that the one you're hoping to get?" Daphne asks.

I realize she's talking to me and I shake my head. "No."

"We're looking for more options, Daphne," my mom says curtly.

"Will you help Elaine make a final decision?" Trina asks her mother.

Daphne shakes her head. "I haven't found the right dress yet. Give me a few minutes and I'll check on her."

"Did you pick this one?" Trina asks, giving me an up and down look at the dress I'm wearing.

Shaking my head, I say, "No. Just trying to find something else."

"Oh good. This one doesn't make you look good at all. I have some options I like. What size do you need?" Trina asks.

"A twelve," I say, avoiding her gaze.

She pulls back the dresses on the rack, reading through the tags. "Do you think you can fit into a ten?"

Without removing a limb, I doubt it. "A twelve would be better." Simple, not rude, but avoiding looking like a sausage in a dress.

She takes four more dresses off the rack and we walk back to the dressing room. At least this store has a variety of sizes.

"I don't think the rose color is a good look for me," I say, pointing to one dress she picked out.

Trina hangs them up in the dressing room and takes out the rose one. "I think you're right. I'm going to check on my sister and then I'll be back to help if you need any."

With how much Trina is running around, she's doing more than the employees of the store.

Once I'm in and struggling to get the zipper down on the dress I've been sporting around the store, I can hear people whispering just outside my room.

"I don't know why you're going through with this. They're going to throw off the whole look of the pictures." Daphne doesn't sound happy.

"Mom, I just want to be happy on my wedding day, to be surrounded by people who support me and Beau. Just because you didn't get the wedding you always wanted doesn't mean you need to be a momzilla."

Inside, I'm conflicted with elation that she would stand up for me and the rest of my family, while also hurt that Daphne would be so cruel.

"I just want it to be perfect for you, dear," Daphne says.

"No, you're trying to control everything. Let me handle this."

I wait several moments before walking out in one dress.

"What do you think?" Trina asks, her expression neutral.

The dress I have on is an empire waist that drapes to the floor. It's actually comfortable and feels good, hiding whatever trouble spots Daphne might think I have.

"I like it."

Trina grins. "I do too. That sage color looks good on you."

Did she just compliment me? Now is not the time to bask in that kind of praise, because it's probably short-lived.

"Better than the rose, for sure," I laugh.

"Do you want to try on any of the others?" she asks.

I shake my head. "Trina, I don't have to be in the bridal party if you don't want me to be." Why am I trying to back out now? As some mental protection against what's coming?

Color drains from her face and she says, "Did you hear my mom?" When I nod, she says, "I apologize for her, Millie. But don't worry about anything she said. I still have a hard time with some things she's tried to instill in me, and I know it will take time. But I think you look beautiful in this. I'm sure Jordan will be speechless. Or are you and Spencer together?"

"What do you mean Jordan?" I feel like I've been punched in the gut.

"Didn't you always have a crush on him?"

"Back in the day," I say. Hopefully my face can convince her I hadn't daydreamed about him from high school until ten days ago, when Spencer and I got closer.

"I think Spencer's a better match for you, anyway." She gives my hands a squeeze.

I wave my hand. "We're just friends. He volunteered to be my date, but I think that's about as far as it goes."

Except for the phone, the spooning in the one bed hotel room, and how his comforting presence always seems to ground me. I like him way too much and I wish he wouldn't just see me as his best friend's little sister. But I don't have time to dwell on that now.

"I don't know. The way he looks at you and how protective he is, I'd say he might have some feelings for you."

"I'm the worst judge of guys and their feelings. So I'm not getting my hopes up."

"Millie, I don't think you understand how great you are. Any guy would be lucky to have you. Don't forget that."

She squeezes my hand and then heads over to help my mom and aunts with their dresses. I walk over to a podium and stand on it, looking at myself in the mirror. This is really flattering. I take out my phone and snap a pic, sending it to Hillary.

Me: This is what I'll be wearing to the wedding.

Hillary: That looks good. Just tell the ladies to take the hem up an inch or two or you'll be tripping all over it.

Me: Personal experience, huh?

Hillary: I tore my Cinderella dress just this morning because of it.

I'm not sure if it's me who's changed or Hillary, but I feel like our relationship has come leaps and bounds from where it was a month ago.

I change into my clothes, carrying the dress over my arm. A couple of stalls away from me, there's another woman just stepping out in a cream dress. I figure she's from another wedding until Trina walks over to confront her.

"This is not the dress you're going to wear," Trina says.

"I won't wear this," the woman says. "I just want something

different that will help me stand out since I'm your maid of honor."

This must be Elaine.

"Then get a different color and try it on." Trina turns away to help one of my aunts hang up the dresses she was carrying in her changing room. Elaine frowns and walks back into the stall next to my aunt.

Who knows when or if I'll have a wedding, but this looks like way more work than I'd want to go through for a wedding. Maybe eloping would be the key to less stress all around.

I think of Spencer and wonder what he'd prefer in a wedding. Being the only child, would he want the whole shebang with weeklong festivities and every activity possible?

28

SPENCER

I glance at my phone again, waiting for any message from Millie. I'm bored to tears in the hotel room I'm sharing with Beau. Getting fitted for our tuxes took all of ten minutes, because they didn't really "fit" them to us. It was more of a "What size are you?" and then hand them out situation. He's watching a basketball game, and I feel like a caged animal who needs to run. Well, not literally.

And the minutes only tick by at a snail's pace.

"Let's do something," I say.

"I didn't sleep much last night. I don't really feel like doing anything."

I frown. Beau has a lot of exceptional qualities, but with this wedding, he's definitely displaying a selfish streak.

"Okay, I'm going to head down to the lobby then. Maybe I'll find something to snack on."

My phone rings as I step outside the room and I smile when I see Jack's name on my screen.

"Jack, how's it going?"

"I'm coming up for air. The other vet has been on a long vacation and I've been covering during the day and the on-call visits. I don't think I've slept over eight hours in the last five days."

I chuckle. That sounds like Jack. "What are you doing talking to me then? You need sleep."

"Do you want to ride over to Miles's? I think they're doing a guys' night tonight. My plan is to nap for a couple of hours and then head over."

"Um, well, I'm actually in Colorado. I thought I sent you a message about that."

I can hear some crackling from his end and then Jack comes back on the line. "Yeah, you did. Sorry about that, man. Good luck with the wedding, though. Are you flying solo?"

"No, Millie is my date."

"Oh, cool. When will you be back? We need to catch up after the past two weeks."

Nodding, I say, "That would be great. I'll keep you updated. I'm not sure what my plans are for the return trip yet." I hadn't thought of that yet. Will Millie want me to drive back with her?

"Sounds good. I'll set us up on a double date or something."

"Huh? Are you feeling okay? I thought you'd sworn off dating after Jessie MacDonald."

Jack groans. "Yeah, well, I might have to do something or you're all going to get married and I'll be the loser who only talks to animals."

"No, I'll probably be the only one left."

"Please," Jack scoffs, "If you'd just hang out with a woman longer than fifteen minutes, and actually let her into your life, you'd be fine. What about Millie?"

"What about her?"

"Well, every time I've talked to you in the past several weeks, you've either had a story about her or you were hanging out with her."

My heart is hammering in my chest. "I think I have feelings for her."

"Great. That's progress, man." Jack's tone isn't bitter, but it's like he already figured that much.

"But, she's Beau's little sister. And she's hung up on some guy from high school."

"Will this guy be at the wedding?"

I nod. "As far as I know."

"Well, then show her that you're better than this guy. You have all the moves to win the girl, you just need to get your head in the right place."

"Thanks, man. Good luck tonight. Tell the guys I'm sorry I missed the hangout."

I hang up and wander to a bar in the lobby and while I'm not in the mood for a drink this early in the day, I need something to do. Anything to keep me from the boredom that is staying in a hotel room all day.

I sit down on a barstool and order a lemonade.

"Spencer Frederickson. It's been a long time."

I turn to see a familiar face, one I haven't seen in over ten years.

Scotty Duncan.

29

SPENCER

S cotty is the last person I ever expected to see in a place like this. He'd been one of my favorite mentors while shooting *The Bright Years* and then I'd been able to play his younger brother on a small mini-series when I was a teen. There's a pang of sadness as I remember the last time I'd seen him. We'd wrapped up shooting for the mini-series and were all meeting at a local restaurant for a small celebratory dinner. He told me to go on ahead and that he'd meet me there.

He never showed up, didn't return my calls or anything. As a sixteen-year-old, it crushed me.

"Scott. It's been a long time." I stand and shake his hand, trying to smile through the pain that's surging. I'd looked up to this man, had seen him as an older brother who had guided me through so many of the obstacles of acting.

"Can I sit?" he asks, pointing to the chair next to where I've been sitting.

I nod and sit back in my seat, wondering why he's here in this town, tucked away in northern Colorado instead of in New York or LA.

"What are you doing here, Scott?" I ask, trying to keep

the frustration out of my voice. There had been so many times when I'd wished I could call and talk to him about what was going on in my life, things I couldn't share with my parents because they just didn't understand as I was trying to adjust to life outside of showbiz. He might not have known from experience, but at least he was always a listening ear.

"I'm here for a wedding, and I hear you are too."

I frown, trying to figure out what he means. "Are you connected to the Burkheads?"

He nods and drums his fingers along the tabletop. "I've been working for their company for the last eight years."

"So this is where you've been since we finished filming? Why'd you leave–?" I cut myself off before I add "me."

"It was time, Spencer. I was involved in some not-good things and just needed to get a fresh start."

Shaking my head, I try to calm my breathing by taking a breath in and letting it out slowly. "I would've understood if you'd just told me. You helped me for so many years, through those times when I got fat-shamed and had braces. But you disappeared."

"Ben Burkhead is my uncle. He took me in after I went to rehab."

"Rehab?" I say, trying to remember any time that I'd seen him not his usual happy self.

Scott nods and says, "Alcohol owned me for so many years, Spence. I didn't want you to see me when I was at my lowest." The guy is only three years older than I am. He must've been a better actor than I thought, because I'd never seen him go overboard with alcohol.

I grit my teeth as I process his words. "A note, a text, something about why you left would've been nice. I had to go through my parents' separation without you, man."

"Last time I talked to your dad, they were still together."

My stomach sinks and I can only whisper, "You've talked to my dad recently?"

He nods. "I call about once a year, just to check in and see how you're doing."

"It wouldn't have been hard to call me."

"I knew how hard you took it when I left, Spence. I just couldn't find the words to say I was sorry and have you understand all that went into my decision."

Standing, I say, "I've got to go. I'll see you around."

I storm up to the room and am glad to see it empty for once. It's like everything I thought I knew about life has turned me around and slapped me in the face. It hurts that Scotty left me out of things when friends should be there. Which brings up Beau leaving our company and ideas to stay here and get married.

Everyone leaves my life at some point. Maybe I'm the problem.

30

MILLIE

I just want to sleep. After a day of trying on dresses, I'm ready to grab a pint of ice cream and binge a show. My parents took the four boys bowling, allowing me a measure of peace for at least an hour.

Once in the room, I pull on some of my comfy pants. A small piece of paper floats out from the bag. I'd written Spencer's list of things to do so I wouldn't forget them and stuffed it into my bag before we left.

Camping got checked off the list sooner than we thought. Drive-in movie will happen before the wedding and we'll be able to work in some others on this trip.

But I'm surprised to see something else scrawled underneath. *Dance with Millie.*

It's a cute sentiment, but I'm surprised by it. Is it something he actually wants to do, or is it for my sake that he's trying to help me? I've got two left feet and the track record to prove it.

Maybe he can teach me something before I embarrass myself completely when we dance at the wedding?

I call Spencer and wait as the ringing sounds over and over. When it goes to voicemail, I decide to hunt him down.

He and Beau are sharing a room at the other end of the hall and I walk down there, dressed in sweats and a pair of flip-flops. I debate whether I should go put on something nicer, a little more fitted to catch Spencer's attention. Because aside from the terror of what dancing in front of a bunch of people is doing to my insides, I'm also hyper aware that my feelings for Spencer are almost past the crush stage.

I take a breath before I knock, suddenly nervous about basically asking him on a date that's not a date.

There's no sound behind the door after I knock, so I call his phone again, only to hear the vibration synced with my phone.

"Spencer! Spence! It's Millie. Open up." I knock a few more times and wait.

The door finally opens, with Spencer squinting because of the brightness of the hallway compared to the darkness of his room.

"Are you sick?" I ask, reaching over to touch his forehead. It feels cool in my palm and I nearly shudder from some weird sensation that goes through me.

"Something like that," he says, walking over and laying on his bed.

"Get up. Let's go do something." I pat his leg and try to get him to move, but he stays still on the bed. So I lay down next to him, our faces only a couple inches away from each other in the darkness.

"What are you doing?" he asks, his words coming out in puffs.

"What are *you* doing?" I ask back. "What happened? Did Beau do something again? I swear, I don't know why you put up with that guy, but I'm glad you did. Or we never would've met."

He lets out a low chuckle. "Are you kidding? Our friends and roommates are all together. Of course we'd have met each other."

We lay there in silence for a few minutes and I can't help

but run my hands through his hair. It must be soothing for him because he closes his eyes.

He says softly, "Are you going to leave me too?"

I pause my movements, trying to make sure I heard what I think. "What do you mean? I'm not going anywhere. But we should go do something. They've got the new Hunter Star movie out. I heard there are some great fight scenes in that one. And then we can stay for The Royal Princess Wedding."

"Is that the sequel?" he asks.

"I think so. It will be fun. Come on." I reach over to grab his arm to drag him off the bed, but he pulls me to him instead. My face is buried next to his chest and I feel warm and protected with his arms around me. A light snore comes out of his mouth and before I know it, I'm drifting off to sleep as well.

If this isn't heaven, I don't want it.

31

SPENCER

I don't know what time it is when Beau finally stumbles into the room, but I'm awake enough to know that there is a body next to me. My brain tries to recall what happened after I came back to the room after seeing Scotty. I took some medicine to curb the headache taking over and then I think I saw Millie at some point.

I stiffen as I now remember her trying to get me to do something. But how did it happen that she's now curled up next to me? Beau is going to kill me.

Reaching over, I gently shake Millie.

"What?" she says in a loud whisper.

I try to put my hand over her mouth to keep her quiet, but my finger ends up jabbing her in the nose.

"What's wrong with you?" Beau mumbles.

"Nothing," I say, trying to sit up casually. "I just need to go to the bathroom."

Millie is sitting up with me now and we both slide off the edge of the bed together. It's still dark and I'm hoping Beau won't notice that my silhouette is wider than normal.

"Why do you have to be so loud?" Beau says, slurring his

words.

"Sorry," I say, and I make it to the bathroom and turn on the light. Millie opens the door as softly as she can and waves as she walks out into the hallway.

I use the facilities and wash my hands before heading back to bed. The clock on the nightstand says four-thirty in the morning.

"You didn't see Millie, did you? Mom was all over me wondering where she went." Beau has his eyes closed and I'm wondering if he's pretending to sleep or just in a drunken stupor.

I freeze and shake my head, even though it's dark in the room now. "I'm not sure where she is. Did she not go back to her room?"

"I don't know. My mom called me seven times asking where she was throughout the night. I thought I'd check with you since you two have been together so much lately."

"Well, I only know you and Millie here. Since you're so busy with your fiancée, it's been fun hanging out with your sister."

"Don't hurt her, man. She gets attached and then can't let go. Then again, if she can get over Jordan Dietrich, it would be a miracle."

His words are like a knife to my chest. I should've realized that. I'm the stand-in for whoever this lifelong crush is. Maybe Millie's idea about being a hermit in the woods is a good idea. Then I don't have to worry about people leaving me. I'll just go crazy talking to myself for the rest of my life.

I think about Scotty Duncan and how he left. I don't think Millie would do that without an explanation, but would I be able to handle it?

It's all I can do to go back to sleep. I've only got a couple more days and then I can head back to Boston and finish what I started with the companies there. I'll marry my work and never get my heart broken again.

32

MILLIE

I'm still riding a wave of adrenaline after leaving Spencer's room early in the morning. We didn't do anything, but if Beau had found out, he would've gone to my parents about it and then there would be the usual Olsen drama, only this time it would be about me.

I know better than to sneak into the family suite this early in the morning, so I head down to the business center and try to stay awake.

My phone has several missed calls and texts from my mom and dad. I'm going to have to come up with a good story as to why I didn't answer. It would be nice to just share that I was helping to comfort Spencer when he was having a hard time, but that wouldn't go over well. My mom would jump to conclusions that we're secretly dating and my dad would probably do a background check and more.

I scroll down and see a missed text in the roomie thread.

Evie: Hey girl! Did you make it to Colorado? We haven't heard from you and wanted to make sure you're okay.

Hillary: I took the last of your chips and bread.

Of course she did.

Dani: Wait, how long are you going to be gone? I was hoping to plan a roomie night out since we've been so busy lately.

It's two hours later in Boston, but I'm surprised they're all up this early.

Kenzie: I have news to share when you get back.

Hillary: You're not going to share it now? We're all on the edges of our seats.

Kenzie: You're still in bed. What are you talking about?

Me: I made it. I'm ready to be home with you all, though.

I reread the messages, loving that despite the unique personalities, we're still able to be close and connected. If only my family could learn that lesson. It's okay to have different opinions and not be made to do every little thing under the guise of being obedient.

I start a new text to Evie, not wanting to share this with everyone.

Me: I think I like Spencer.

Not even seconds later, a response pops up.

Evie: I knew it. You two are great together. Have you kissed yet?

Me: Chances of that happening are slim, Eves. And I'm not sure, but I think Beau gave him an ultimatum that he shouldn't hang out with me or something.

Evie: Spencer can think for himself. Enjoy this time, girl. And send pictures of the two of you!

I must've fallen asleep next to the computer in the business room because the next thing I know, my phone is ringing at 7:02 am. It's my mother.

"Hi Mom," I say, trying to come up with a story, and fast. Everything is a little fuzzy, especially since I never took out my contacts last night.

"Where have you been? We've been so worried about you!" In the background, I can hear my father's loud snores. I'm sure he's really torn up about my disappearance.

"I was out catching up with my roommates and fell asleep in the business center," I say, which is all true.

"We have a full day ahead. Get up here and get ready. We're supposed to be at the brunch meeting in a couple hours."

"Brunch with whom?" I ask, walking toward the elevators.

"With everyone in the wedding party. Jordan should be there."

I groan. If there's anything I've learned from the last week, it's that I no longer need the mythical fantasy of Jordan Dietrich to get me through my life. Spencer is all that and more.

"I'm over him, Mom. Please don't do anything embarrassing."

She laughs and says, "Sometimes children need a push to get their love life started."

Oh, please let that not be a sign of what's to come.

Two and a half hours later, after a lecture on letting them know where I am at all times, I'm in a large ballroom at the resort, dressed in an A-line skirt and a floral blouse. They were options snuck from Evie's closet, and I'm glad I brought them, not knowing how many events we were going to be part of.

I see Spencer across the room, and while he looked good in Beau's old clothes while we camped, he looks even better in his normal polished casual look. It doesn't sound like that should be a thing, but it is for Spencer.

Frank groans next to me as he sees all the adults. "Can't there just be a big playground to run around, or even a gaming center where all the kids can just stay out of the way?" He winks at me and I laugh, knowing if there was such a thing as a gaming room, I'd hide out there too.

"If only it were that easy," I say. I'm not sure where to start or what I'm supposed to do. Trina hasn't given me any instructions on what she expects of me as a bridesmaid, so am I supposed to mingle at this thing? Or can I just sit down and hope it will end swiftly?

"Hey, isn't that the kid you crushed on forever?" Eric says, leaning closer to me and pointing toward Spencer. Sure enough, Jordan walks over and stands next to Spencer and Beau.

He looks nearly the same as he did in high school, except for the already thinning hair up front. "Jordan? Yeah, that's him."

Eric gives me a frown and says, "Why aren't you swooning at the sight of him?"

I roll my eyes. "I did that once, and it was because I hadn't eaten all day."

"So, what about now?" Frank asks. "Are you going to kiss him?"

I cringe and shake my head. "No. And I'm not talking about that kind of stuff with you gomers. Go find some food. Maybe make a disturbance so we can leave this event early."

"Will you back us up if we do?" Eric asks, the mischievous side of him already plotting.

Nodding, I say, "Sure. I'll take the heat if it comes to that."

The boys high five each other and run off. But now I'm standing awkwardly alone. I glance over at Spencer and Jordan. The height difference is significant and while I can see what I liked in Jordan all those years ago, I'm firmly Team Spencer right now. If only he could like me back.

In a moment of bravery, I walk over to where the boys are standing and stop next to Spencer. He glances down and gives me wide eyes before a big smile. He must've remembered about our nighttime adventure.

"Hey Millie," Beau says, "You're alive. I thought Mom was going to have a heart attack if she didn't find you."

I give him a smile and say, "I'm alive and present. How many more of these activities do we have to attend?"

"At least five more, I think," Jordan says next to me. "You're Millie? You've definitely grown up."

Just what every girl wants to hear.

"It's nice to see you, Jordan." I'm not sure what else to say. He's definitely not aged as well as my imagination painted him from five years ago, but he still seems nice. "What brings you to the wedding?"

"He's one of my groomsmen," Beau says.

"Have you been friends for long?" I ask, curious when this friendship started.

"We started hanging out after Beau graduated college and came back," Jordan says with a small smile.

"Cool," is all I can think to say. I turn to Spencer and say, "How are you this morning?"

Surprise mixed with confusion crosses his features. "Um, good."

It's vague and short, which isn't like Spencer. He usually gives a thorough description of everything he does.

There's a tapping of a microphone and we all turn to see Mr. Burkhead over by the small platform stage.

"Welcome everyone. Thank you for coming to this small celebration for my daughter. We're getting used to the idea of her being married to Beau, but we hope they have a life they've always dreamed of." It might be just me, but it sounds like he's trying to send his daughter a coded message.

"Go ahead and mingle, get some food, and then head outside for some lawn activities."

"That should make the boys happy," I mumble.

Spencer leans over and whispers, "What?"

"Eric and Frank wanted to play. I think they'll be happy now."

"Me too, if it gets me out of this room." His gaze focuses on something across the room, and I turn to follow it. There's a guy there, but I've never seen him before.

"Who's that?" I ask, tuning out the rest of Trina's dad's speech. Wasn't the invitation to eat and head outside a signal for the end of his talking?

Spencer glances down at me. "Scotty Duncan, a guy I used to work with."

"Here?" I now remember the guy Spencer avoids talking about. "That's great. You should go talk to him."

He shakes his head. "I'm good. Did you get some food already?"

I loop my arm through his and say, "Not yet. Let's go get a few things and see what activities they have for us." Approaching the topic of Spencer's old coworker is going to have develop slowly.

Once we'd walk away, Spencer leans over and says, "Good job on that. Jordan watched you walk away with me."

I blink several times, trying to figure out what he means. "It's funny when you see someone after a long time. It's like your memories were a bit off on them." I turn to see Jordan in a chugging contest with Beau.

Spencer points toward Jordan. "You're not fantasizing about that guy anymore?"

I laugh and say, "Nope. Chalk it up to no longer being a teenager in a small town."

For the first time since I've seen him this morning, he relaxes somewhat. We get a plate and load up some of the mini sandwiches and fruit spread out on the table. "Man, they're really putting a lot of money into this event. Have you always dreamed about a big wedding? Or something small?"

"To be honest, I haven't really gotten that far." I take a small cup of orange juice and wait for him to get the last of what he needs before we walk outside.

"You haven't spent every waking moment of your life planning your wedding?" Spencer teases.

I chuckle and say, "I haven't. Living with my family has

taught me a lot of the dos and don'ts with money, and I just think that if it could be a chill day where everyone had fun and it wasn't all about the extravagance and the appearance, that it would be worth it. Why spend tens of thousands on a day, or several days in this case, when you'll have the rest of your life with your spouse?"

Spencer says nothing and smiles, looking at me like I'm an anomaly.

"I know. It sounds lame."

"No, not lame."

The lawn outside is set up with several activities: horseshoes, bow and arrow shooting at targets, and other games my brothers are wholeheartedly taking part in. Spencer leads me to the side and we take a seat on a bench.

"Are you okay?" I ask. Spencer's gaze seems to be glazed over.

"Yeah," he says, shaking out of it.

"Okay, so the guy inside used to work with you," I say, trying to get the story started. It has to be why his mood is so different from his usually bubbly self.

Spencer nodded. "He left without saying goodbye. We were really good friends, like brothers, and he disappeared until now."

I can feel the betrayal in his words. "I'm so sorry. Why is he here, though?"

"He's Trina's cousin, I think." Spencer takes a bite of his food before he says, "So, this Jordan guy. He's not quite what I pictured him to be."

Laughing, I say, "You were trying to picture him?"

"Well, I was curious what guys you were into. Tall, short, bald, etc." He grins at me, but it's not as mischievous as it usually is.

"My list has changed in the past few months." More like days, but I don't want to call attention to anything and ruin our relationship if he doesn't have feelings for me. I'd rather live in the friend zone than not have Spencer in my life because he feels awkward around me.

"Oh, really?" Spencer glances around the field and points to an older guy with a beer belly. "How about that guy?"

I laugh and say, "He's old for me, and he's probably my second cousin, once removed."

"That's right. I forget you're kind of related to everyone here."

"Not everyone, but many people. Now do you wonder why I booked it to Boston?"

Spencer nods and glances around again. "That must be so weird to have that many family members. My extended family is tiny."

"There are advantages and disadvantages, I guess."

We finish up our plates of food and Spencer reaches over for my paper plate. He gets up and throws mine and his into a trash can.

"What should we do first?" he asks.

"How about lawn bowling? That looks fun."

He grins at me and reaches for my hand, pulling me gently along with him. "Let's do it."

His palm is warm and he doesn't let go after a few feet. I hope he's not trying to put on a show for Jordan. That guy is in the past and I would love nothing more than for Spencer to be my future.

33

SPENCER

As the best man, there are duties I have to perform. Like planning the bachelor party. There were some stipulations put to me by Trina, which I wasn't planning to get anyway for this party. A bachelor party should be the groom hanging out with his friends doing whatever it is he wants before the wedding takes place. Not tempting him to stay in the bachelor category.

Trina's sister, Elaine, wasn't excited to be doing a joint party and even less excited for a drive-in theater.

"That's so ghetto. Why can't we go to a nice dinner and then hit the bars?" she said.

It took several negotiation tactics after the garden party the day before for her to finally agree. Basically, Trina told her that's what we should do.

We've lined up several vehicles to come and Millie's brother, Carl, went home to get camping and beanbag chairs, along with an enormous pile of blankets.

We get to the drive-in and I can't wait to experience this. I've already survived camping outdoors on this trip. Watching a movie outside should be fun, like a stamp in an adventure passport.

Once we get there, Elaine goes up to Trina and says, "Remember, this was your idea of fun. I didn't want to do this on your last outing as a single woman."

Trina shrugs. "Why not? We haven't done this since we were kids. It'll be fun. We've got drinks and snacks, plus a front row seat to the movie."

"Where do you want to sit?" I ask Millie. "Since you are the more experienced driver-inner, where should I sit to get the maximum view of the screen?"

She laughs and I love that sound, wishing I could help her do that as often as possible. "Let's take a bean bag before the others get there."

She scrambles up into the bed of the truck and lies down on the beanbag, patting the space next to her. When I sit down, we kind of slide together in the middle of the bag. We adjust, but it's still like we're cuddling. I don't mind it, but I don't want her to be weirded out.

"Do you need me to move some more?" I ask. My chin is resting on the top of her head with my arm wrapped around her back.

Beau glances up at us and frowns. "No making out with my sister."

Millie's body tenses up and I'm not sure if it's because she's embarrassed about his comment or the thought of us kissing.

I wave Beau away and remember the one thing I forgot to bring out of the truck. I'd worked to hide it so it would be a surprise for my date to this shindig.

I squirm back out of the beanbag and run to grab the black padded case from inside the truck. Then I hop up into the bed of the truck again, holding it out to Millie.

"What's this?" she says, looking confused.

"A present for the night. I had to borrow it because I didn't think of the idea until too late."

She glances up at me with a "you-shouldn't-have" look and undoes the zipper. "A camera?"

I nod, trying to read her expression. "I thought it would be fun for you to take a few pictures tonight. If only I'd thought about it before, I could've bought one for you."

"You already bought me a phone." Millie says, shaking her head. "Who did you borrow this from?"

"That's my little secret. Go take some pics and then come back and we'll enjoy the movie."

Millie looks giddy as she fiddles with the buttons and dials on the camera. She moves in several angles, taking pictures of the horizon. The sun has already set, but there's still a bit of muted light and I can't wait to see how the picture comes out.

She gathers up the group and snaps a picture, then goes around to take pictures in smaller groups. When she gets back to the beanbag, my cheeks hurt from smiling so much.

Millie slides next to me and holds the camera out to take a picture. With our faces close together, I smile. Man, I don't think I've ever been this excited to sit close to another woman. We're basically a tangle of arms in this beanbag, but it's even better that Millie is all smiles.

"Say cheese," she says, before pushing the button to take the picture. She turns the camera around right after, checking the screen. "You blinked and I only got half of my face on that one."

"Selfies on these cameras are a lot harder."

She lifts the camera again and takes another photo. As she's studying the screen, I'm tempted to tilt her head back and kiss her soundly. As a lesson, of course. But then again, do I want to do that when her brother could just look back and see everything? And a first kiss here is not ideal.

For Millie's sake, I have to stay strong and just pretend like we're good buddies. Even though everything inside me is screaming to move from best friend's little sister to girlfriend.

34

MILLIE

I can't help but keep staring at the picture of me and Spencer for several minutes before the movie starts. Okay, so I have to go back and forth through the other photos I've taken so I don't look like a stalker while sitting this close to him, but I've almost imprinted the photo into my mind with how many times I've looked at it.

The tilt of our heads and the bright smiles are nearly picture perfection. I put the camera back in the case once the movie starts and cuddle up with Spencer. I'm feeling brave, so I might as well embrace it.

"Are you warm?" Spencer asks, pulling a blanket up and over my shoulders.

"I'm good. You?"

He gives me a small smile and says, "I'm happy."

That seems like an unusual answer to physical comfort, but I'm just going to let it slide and enjoy this night. I stare at his lips too long, wondering what it would be like to kiss him. I have no prior experience in the kissing department, and fear holds me back.

What if I'm a terrible kisser? What if Spencer is just the

nicest guy in the world and doesn't actually have feelings for me?

Several people are asleep by the time the second feature begins, including Spencer. I lift my hand to run through his hair over and over, enjoying the feel of his soft locks through my hands.

What am I going to do about this guy? He's like a knight on a white horse with all his gestures and kindness. My phone, the hotel rooms, finding me this camera for the night. Not one man in my family would've done anything close to this. And yet, I've given him nothing.

He deserves something for his kindness, but what?

35

SPENCER

The drive-in movie was great until I fell asleep. It must've been the several days of driving and the lack of sleep on the camping trip, but I was exhausted.

Now, early the next morning, as we listen to the instructor in the dancing class we've been assigned, I can see Millie is anxious about something, because she's practically biting her fingernail off.

"What's up?" I whisper.

She turns to me with a look of confusion and then drops her hand to her side. "Nothing. Just trying to understand what I'm supposed to do."

"About?"

She sighs and waves at her brother and Trina, standing next to the instructor. "Dancing. I'm the worst. That Trina could get any of the Olsen men in this room is some kind of miracle."

I laugh, glancing around the room at each of them. Father Olsen keeps trying to adjust the sport coat he's wearing, as if he's completely uncomfortable with it. Being a car salesman, I would think he'd have to wear nicer attire daily, but maybe he never puts on more than a colored shirt and tie.

Beau looks just as nervous, but he keeps smiling at Trina, like he's hoping she'll be able to guide him through whatever the instructor asks.

Carl, Danny, Eric, and Frank are all paired up with either single women in the families, or female teenagers. I'm not sure which family they're from, but Frank isn't looking happy about being here at all. Bribery was involved just to get him in the door.

The music begins, and I take Millie's hand in mine. I adjust her hand on my shoulder and then move my free hand to her waist, channeling all the information I remember from classes as a teen. We'd had several dancing scenes for the show I was on at the time since I played a competitive ballroom dancer, and there were a lot of backstage lessons to get me to a believable talent level.

I count softly, trying to get her to understand the steps.

She frowns at me and says, "Don't tell me you're good at this, too."

I laugh and shake my head. "It was a necessary skill."

"And then you got stuck with me," she says. It's then that her heel comes down and slams into my foot, causing me to jerk back and wince. "I'm so, so sorry."

Shaking it off, I say in a strangled voice, "You're fine." Once I catch my breath, stand up and prepare myself again. She looks terrified and that she's going to severely injure me. I might get some bumps and bruises, but if I can take away some of her anxiety, I can handle it.

"You've got to learn somehow, right? Just picture a box in your head. When my right foot takes a step back, your left foot goes forward to follow it. Then we'll take a step to your right, and then you'll take a step back."

We move slowly, and there are a few times she hesitates as she focuses on what foot should go where, but she's getting the motion of it.

"Did you ever go to a dance at school?" I ask, suddenly curious.

She nodded. "Once. It was the junior year girls ask dance."

"Oh, so you have some experience with asking a guy out," I say with a teasing grin.

Millie rolls her eyes. "I didn't have to ask him face to face. It was through candy and a fun saying. Which made things extra awkward in the halls at school until he finally answered me."

"How did you dance with him?"

"There was no real dancing. It was the arms around the neck, swaying back-and-forth kind of thing. But I think there were only two slow dances. The rest were line dances or the faster, more popular songs, so everyone would just jump up and down to the music."

She steps on my foot again, but just barely this time.

"Look at that, you're improving."

With a burst of laughter, she says, "Improving? I still stepped on your foot."

"Yeah, but only two of my toes were damaged in the collision."

She laughs again, and for the second time in twenty-four hours, I'm tempted to lean in and kiss her. But something keeps holding me back.

I try to analyze that as we keep dancing, my body on autopilot. She's already admitted that she isn't as interested in the Jameson guy as she was when we were heading out here. And it's not like Beau will maim me for dating his sister, will he?

My brain can't quite catch onto the niggling feeling inside. Maybe it's because she's so young. Then again, she's only three and a half years younger than me. Her inexperience with dating? No, because everyone has their first time in love. If we date, would I be the backup because she's liked that guy for years?

The music changes and I realize everyone else has stopped for some more instruction from the teacher.

"Did you get lost in that big brain of yours for a second?" Millie asks with a laugh.

"Just a bit," I say, chuckling.

"What were you thinking about?" she asks, staring up at me.

"You," I say.

36

MILLIE

My heart stops. He's thinking about me? My inner sixteen-year-old is screaming right now.

Spencer blinks and then shakes his head before he says, "I mean, how far you've come on this trip." The music begins again, and he guides me gently.

I make a sound to let him know he's crazy and then say, "I don't think there's been that much change. I've worked on saying no twice."

"True," Spencer says, his lips turning into a slight frown. "But that's still more than it would've been, right?"

I glance around and say, "Yes."

With a laugh, Spencer says, "Progress. Look how much you're improving here."

For the first time in forever, I'm blushing. Full-on, awkward heat rushing to my cheeks. The guy is the most handsome man I've ever seen, which is only enhanced by what I know about him.

"So, how are you doing?" I say, trying to figure out where his headspace is now.

"Is that a pickup line? Or just a check in on me moment?"

Spencer winks at me and I'm trying to figure out what he means.

Before I can form a coherent, semi-normal sentence, my mouth blurts out, "Both!"

Terror courses through my chest. How am I going to survive this? He's going to get a strange look on his face and then try to politely avoid me until the end of time.

Instead, he laughs and twirls me around, catching me in his arms just as the music is ending. If I didn't have a huge crush on the guy already, I would now.

Our noses are inches away, and his chest is rising and falling quickly. Clapping from the front of the room has Spencer lifting me back to a standing position as the instructor walks toward us.

"Well done. I could feel the tension in the dance. You'll be the perfect couple to follow the bride and groom."

"Shouldn't the maid of honor be dancing with the best man?" Elaine asks. She walks over from where she was dancing and stands in front of Spencer, her face beaming with hope. The instructor had just asked everyone to find a partner at the beginning of the class, and I hadn't even thought of what the tradition is for normal weddings.

"You're not the maid of honor?" the instructor asks me.

With my heart sinking in my chest, I shake my head. "I'm just a bridesmaid."

The instructor's smile falters a bit, before he replaces it and says, "Let's try it again, with the two of you together." He points to Elaine and Spencer and as much as I want to scream that Spencer is my date, I nod and take a step back.

When I turn to walk toward my brother, not wanting to see Spencer's hands and arms around another woman, I search for another partner. My brother, Carl, already has a partner. I'm not sure who she is or why she's here, since this is a practice just for the bridal party, but I might as well sit this one out.

"Do you need a partner?" a male voice asks from behind me. I turn to find Jordan standing there with his hand outstretched. "I doubt I'll be as graceful as that other guy, but I'd hate for you to sit by yourself during the practice."

I have no desire to dance with anyone but Spencer. Then again, there are a couple of my cousins who are sitting on the sideline I'd have to be paired up with if I don't accept Jordan.

"Sure," I say, taking his outstretched hand. It could be worse. I could be paired up with one of my brother's other groomsmen, a couple of which look like they're getting handsy with their partners.

I put my hand on Jordan's shoulder and he puts his hand up high enough on my side that he's an inch from my armpit. Well, at least he isn't trying anything else.

"So, what's life like in Boston?" he asks. His steps are stiff, and it feels like everything I worked on with Spencer is reverting to the awkwardness of thirty minutes ago.

"I love it there. Boston has so much to do and it's been nice to kind of grow into my own person, although I think that's a thing in progress." I pause and give him a small smile. "I remember you saying that you like to travel. Have you been anywhere fun in the past few years?"

He gives me a side glance and says, "I said that?"

Why did I bring that up? "Someone knocked over all my books in high school and you helped me pick them up. We chatted for a minute and you showed me a book about traveling the world and how much you wanted to explore."

Again with the word vomit. I guess that's better than freezing up completely. I'm going from one end of the awkward social spectrum to the other. Maybe someday I'll end up safely in the middle.

"That's crazy that you remember something from that long ago. Yeah, I always wanted to see Egypt and the pyramids. I haven't made it there yet."

"I'm sure it takes a lot to get there, but saving always helps." I'm hoping my words are more encouraging than anything.

"Yeah, I have a really hard time saving money. I just spent what I had on the latest PlayStation console. That's where I travel the most these days."

It takes some effort to keep the horrified expression off my face. Not that I'm against video games, because as a woman with five brothers, I've played my fair share of them, but settling for seeing the world through them? It's like the fake version of life.

"What about you? Are you thinking of staying in the northeast? You should come back home and we could hang out more."

Shaking my head, I say, "Yeah, I think I'll be there for the foreseeable future. I'm hoping to travel a bit more over there and maybe head on a cruise someday." I'm not sure where that came from. Cruises are up there with planes on my fear list.

Jordan gives me a small smile. "You should fly to Europe. I've talked to some of my online friends from over there and they say it's cheap to travel once you're over there."

"I'll have to think about it." That would involve flying and not for just a short puddle jump trip.

Is this song ever going to end? We are basically swaying in place and I can see Spencer out of the corner of my eye now. He still looks just as graceful with his steps, but his face seems so serious, compared to what it was with me a few minutes ago. Or am I just trying to make myself feel better?

Once the dancing is done, the instructor says a few more things and then we're finally released. I say thank you to Jordan for the dance and hurry to get my bag and phone.

I turn to see Spencer walking over, giving me a smile that doesn't quite reach his eyes. "How'd it go with Juan Diego?"

His comment makes me laugh loudly, causing the rest of

the room to turn toward me. I duck my head and focus on the floor for a moment until they all look elsewhere.

"It was eye-opening."

"What do you mean by that?" he asks.

I try to think of a way to describe it. "Do you want to get some lunch?"

Spencer smiles and nods. "As long as you're going to share the gossip."

"Done."

37

SPENCER

I don't know what I thought Ruby's diner would look like before, but this place is straight out of the 1960s. The booth benches are covered in a flowered color fabric that reminds me of a dress my grandmother used to wear when I was a kid.

"This is different," I say, sliding into the booth across from Millie. I would've liked to be close to her again after our dance, but I don't want to weird her out. And I've made fun of every other couple who sit on the same side of the bench since I was a teenager.

"It's fun. They serve a large variety of foods and it's the place I would go a lot after school."

"Did you come here with friends?" I ask.

Her smile fades. "No, I worked here from ninth grade to after graduation, first as a busser and then as a server. I'd find a seat in the back and do my homework until my shift started."

I feel bad that I brought it up. I've never heard her talk about friends from high school.

"That's cool that you had a job like that. I always wanted to try being a waiter."

We give our order to the server, and then I lean forward, trying to tease a bit. "So, about this eye-opening experience you had. Tell me about it."

Millie laughs and says, "Have you ever thought you wanted something, and you dream about it and think about it, and it just doesn't meet your expectations? It was like that."

Something about that makes me grin. I'd been trying to hold in my disappointment at having to swap Millie for Elaine. She kept trying to make eye contact with me, flirting about any little move or thing in the room. I did everything I could to evade that, but it was hard not to watch Millie and her dance partner.

"It seems I've trained you well, young Padawan." I take a sip of the Sprite the server brings and watch her reaction.

She gives me a quick smile and says, "Yes, yes you have. Jordan ended up doing the high school sway halfway through the song."

"How many more events do we have for this wedding?" I ask, trying to get another laugh out of her.

"I don't even know. I'm ready to be home."

"What is the difference between being here or in Boston?"

She blows out a long breath and then says, "Everything. Here, it will take a lot of time to break out of the roles I've held for a long time. Sure, we've made some progress, but there's still work to be done. In Boston, I can live my life, believe in my own opinions, and work on my own to get where I want to go. Although this week has been worth it to 'earn' the money for my rent."

I'm still blown away that she had to do that.

"What about you? How are you taking the idea that Beau won't be there to help run the company?"

It's a simple question, one that I've thought about periodi-cally since that phone call from Beau saying he was getting married, but I still don't have a definitive answer on how I feel about that.

"I wish he would be there. We've been through a lot together, and we did a lot to get everything ready for launch. I'm just surprised he would go for something like recruiting when he's got way more experience as an actor."

Millie raises her eyebrow. "Are you sure about that?"

"What do you mean?"

"He's never had a part in a movie or commercial that lasts longer than ten seconds. But he played baseball for several years before heading to college. As strange of a U-turn as he's taken in his life, maybe he really feels like that's the sweet spot for him."

I hadn't thought of it in those terms and I'm again surprised by Millie's wisdom. She doesn't think she's knowledgeable, but she's pointed out things that I never would've considered had she not brought them up.

"So, you think it's good?" I study her face, noting how she glances away to gain composure before facing me again.

"In a weird way, yeah. I mean, this whole thing is crazy anyway, with him marrying Trina. But if he's comfortable doing what he's doing, then there's nothing wrong with that. As long as he doesn't border on illegal."

The food comes out and I'm surprised at how good my burger is. There aren't too many varieties of hamburgers in the world, but this one hits the spot.

"I can tell why you like this place. This is amazing."

Millie picks up one of the sweet potato fries and dunks it into a light orange sauce. "It's the best. If only we could take this restaurant and transplant it to Boston. Life would be complete."

We finish the meal and I pick up the check, much to Millie's chagrin. We head out and walk down the street, with Millie pointing out a few things she remembers from growing up.

"We'd come up here on weekends to hang out. I'd drive my

brothers up here once I got a license and we'd get an ice cream or something to survive the summer heat. Over there is where I lost my wallet that had a lot of money I'd saved for a new computer in it. Jordan found it and returned it to me."

"Oh, so you have reasons for picturing him as the white knight," I say, with some humor.

"He's a very nice guy, just not hitting all the boxes now."

I tuck my hands into my pants pockets and say, "What are all those boxes?"

Her cheeks blossom with a bright red color and I wonder if I said something wrong. It's happened.

"I'm not sure, to be honest. It's just something my room-mates say."

"So you don't have a set of criteria for a guy you'd like to date?"

Shaking her head, she says, "Remember, I said I don't want to wish for the wrong things. What about you?"

"What traits will check my boxes?" I ask, taking a long look at her before staring forward again. "I think a few of them have changed recently."

I could list it off for her, everything from the red hair to the knowledge about so many things she doesn't deem important. Like how much she knows about trucks and road trips and snacks. The relationship she has with her brothers and how strong she is to face her fears. And how she's willing to forgive someone who wronged her for so long when she didn't have to. What's not to like about this woman walking next to me?

It's not lost on me that her relationship with Trina is like mine with Scotty aside from the high school bullying. I'm just not ready to get over the betrayal yet.

"Well, now you've got me curious," she says to me, pulling me out of my thoughts. I must give her a strange look because she says, "Boxes?"

"Amelia!" The voice causes us to turn. Across the street is

someone waving at us. Millie groans next to me and that makes me panic, even though I don't recognize the woman.

She's a shorter woman and she doesn't even check for cars before darting across the road to stand in front of us. To her credit, this isn't Boston. Pedestrians have the right of way there, but it's always wise to still check and make sure that a car is going to stop.

"Aunt Marge, it's so nice to see you." Millie's smile is forced and she inches closer to me. I'm not complaining.

"You too, Amelia." She turns to me and says, "Hi, I've heard all about you. You must be Jordan."

I cough, trying to mask a laugh, and after a quick glance at Millie, she's horrified. I take the woman's outstretched hand, and she pulls me in for what I could only term as a bear hug. When the woman finally pulls back, I can see the embarrassment in Millie's expression.

"I hope it's only good things you've heard."

"He's not Jordan," Millie says, her eyes flashing. "I wish my family would realize that I've moved on from that. This is Spencer Frederickson."

Her words surprise me and there's a zip of excitement running through me at the thought that maybe she's talking about me.

"Oh, Beau's actor friend?" She steps closer and pulls me down to where I'm only about two inches from her face. "You know, I used to watch you on *The Bright Years*. It's so great to see you here supporting my nephew. You'll have to come over to my house and meet my daughter. She's so accomplished at everything, and I think you two would really hit it off."

Millie wasn't lying earlier when she said her family would try to set me up. "I appreciate that, but I'm here with Millie."

That's the first time I've seen the woman actually take a breath in the few moments I've known her.

"Were you on the camping trip?" I ask, curious.

Aunt Marge shakes her head. "No, that's just for the Olsen side. I'm part of the Scheiners."

I turn to Millie for an explanation and she says, "My mom's side."

Nodding, I turn back to the woman with a smile. "That's probably why we didn't meet before. It's been nice to see you, but we were heading over here for, um, what was it again, Millie?"

A panicked expression crosses her face before she replaces it with a more confident one. "Checking on the flowers. Beau and Trina asked us to check and make sure they were ready for tomorrow."

Aunt Marge nods and I'm grateful for Millie's quick thinking.

"That's very important. Well, good luck to you two. Let me know if I can help. We'll see you tomorrow." She walks away but turns back to us. "I just can't believe Beau is getting married, and this quickly, too. I thought my daughter, Bernice, would be married before him, but she's got her condition, you know."

I don't know, but I won't say anything that might jeopardize when she'll stop talking.

"We're all surprised by the sudden nuptials," Millie says, nodding. I think she'll say something else, but she's staring at her aunt, as if willing her to stop talking.

"And to marry a Burkhead, of all people. Sharla and Daphne had been so close until the whole dance fiasco. I'll never forget when Daphne attacked Sharla at school because she got picked and Daphne didn't."

I nod, glancing around for any excuse to get out of this conversation. The woman seems nice, but I might lose a week of my life rehashing the past with her.

Millie grabs my hand and says, "Thanks, Aunt Marge. We're already late."

She tugs me a few steps down the sidewalk and we both wave at Aunt Marge.

The woman waves back and calls out, "Save a dance for Bernice tomorrow. I'm sure she'll be ecstatic."

We make it another block before Millie bursts out laughing, the kind that is catching, making me follow along.

"I can't believe she would do that. Oh wait, she's my aunt. I can totally believe she'd try to set you up with my cousin."

"What is with the women in your family trying to set me up?"

She pauses for a moment and turns to look at me. "Well, you're a good-looking guy who lives in Boston and you're single. Those are the only requirements needed for meddling mothers."

"What about your mother?" I ask, curious why Sharla has never done the same.

"I don't know. She does it in her own way, I think. I'm grateful, or else I would've never been able to show my face here again. I can't imagine having to date most of the guys in this area without awkward consequences."

"You've been anything but awkward with me," I say, turning toward her and reaching up to hold her arms.

She smiles and says, "You're a unique case."

It's like a magnet is pulling me forward and I can't stop looking at her lips as I lean in. We're almost a breath away when a car horn startles Millie, and she takes a step back.

"We should probably get back to the resort," she says. "Maybe we can try out the pool."

I nod, trying to regain my composure as she takes my hand again and tugs me back down the sidewalk. It's a walk to get to the resort, but maybe I can get my feelings to simmer down for the woman holding my hand.

38

MILLIE

It's getting harder to keep from revealing my feelings for Spencer. We were millimeters from kissing and I went and ruined it by jumping back. If only I could go back and redo that. Then again, would my lack of experience in that department turn him off?

And we survived Aunt Marge, which is saying something. I'm grateful Spencer keeps sticking up for me, even when people can't believe he would be here with me. The guy is off the charts attractive, and I'm more of a plain Jane.

But if there is any hope that I could make this work, it will have to be when I'm out of this town and away from my meddling family. I worry every time we meet a relative that Spencer is going to head straight for the airport and conveniently lose my phone number. The poor guy doesn't have much extended family and is an only child, so to have to deal with both sides of my crazy family is something.

My father is asleep on the bed and my mother is next to him with a rag on her forehead, meaning she's got a headache. The boys are in the adjoining common room, the TV on with the volume up to at least a hundred.

"Why don't you tell them to turn it down?" I ask, having to shout so she can hear me.

"I have. They won't listen." My mom's lips pinch shut, and I know she's in serious pain. She gets migraines from time to time, usually when she's extra stressed and I'm sure the noise isn't helping things. I walk into the other room and take the remote from Danny, turning it down.

"Hey, we're watching that," Danny says, pointing to the TV.

"And you can still watch it, just at a manageable volume. You're all going to be deaf if you keep the sound up that loud."

The four of them frown at me, but they're back to glued to the movie playing. I close the door as I walk back into the other side of the room. The sound isn't blaring like it was before.

Feeling bold, I shake my dad's leg, trying to wake him up. "What?" he barks.

"Mom has a migraine and the kids are being loud. You won't help her?"

He sits up, rubbing his eyes. It takes a few moments, but he glances over at his wife. "What's wrong?"

"I forgot my meds," my mom says with her eyes closed.

"What do you want me to do?" Dad asks, sounding irritated.

Shaking my head, I say, "Go find her some medicine or take the kids out of here. She waits on you all the time. The least you can do is help her when she's not feeling well."

My dad stands and walks over to me. I'm suddenly not feeling as bold as I was moments ago.

"Is that what you think?" he asks, glaring at me with pinched lips.

I hesitate a moment before nodding.

He blows out a breath and says, "Let's take the boys out. I'll find some medicine for Mom."

I march into the other room and say, "Get your suits on. We're going to the pool."

That sets off a chain of more yelling as three of the four fight to get to the bathroom first to change.

"Aren't you coming, Carl?"

He's frowning and says, "She hasn't responded yet."

I'm confused about who he's talking about and then think back to the dance class this morning. "The girl you were dancing with?"

He nods and glances back at his phone again. "She said she'd call when we got back to the hotel so we could hang out."

I pat his shoulder and say, "It's all right, Carl. Maybe she had to do something first. There is a lot to get figured out for the wedding tomorrow."

"I know, but I don't want to be alone forever."

It takes all the willpower I possess to not laugh out loud. He's barely eighteen and worried about this?

"You'll be fine. Get your swimsuit on and let's go get some sun. Maybe she'll text you then. Sometimes it's better to do something than to keep watching a pot waiting for it to boil."

Carl frowns and shakes his head. "You sound like Mom, bruh."

"Well, that's how I feel when I come here." I turn and head back in to get my swimsuit on and then round up the group, grateful we have at least a football to play with in the water.

"We're heading to the pool," I tell my mother. "Dad should be back soon with some medicine. Call me if he doesn't come back in ten minutes."

She nods her head and then grimaces.

"Thank you, Amelia," she says in a weak whisper.

"You should stand up for yourself, Mom," I say. "He should take care of you when you're unwell."

"It's no use, Millie. Sometimes we have to just grin and bear it."

I head out with the boys, thinking about her words. Being resigned in a relationship is not something I want. Ever.

Spencer is grabbing a towel from the poolside station and smiles when he sees the surrounding chaos. "Looks like you've got an entourage there."

I nod and shake my head. "More like a boy mob. Hey, come get sunscreen on." The boys all groan, but each of them stops and waits for me to spray them with the stuff.

Once they're all in the pool, Spencer takes their spot, arms out and his eyes and mouth closed.

I raise an eyebrow. "You want me to spray you with sunscreen?" It's then that I take in his toned chest and arms for the second time on this trip. The guy is hot.

He laughs and shakes his head. "No, I just thought it would be funny to add me to your boy mob." He reaches out for the can of sunscreen and I give it to him. "Turn around."

I frown, trying to figure out what he needs. Is he going to spray sunscreen in some random spot?

"I'll get your back so you don't burn."

That feels a lot more intimate than I would've thought before, but I turn, moving my braid out of the way. The sunscreen is cold against my skin, but what's more shocking is that Spencer rubs it into my skin. Then he massages my shoulder, making me so relaxed I could probably fall asleep standing here.

"You okay?" Spencer asks, his lips right next to my ear and sending a shiver through me.

"Yep," I say, spinning away from him. "Let me help you with the sunscreen."

I don't know what's changed, but there's definitely something between us. But can we bridge the little gap without me messing it up?

39

SPENCER

I might've gotten a little carried away with the sunscreen and massage. Yes, that's not helping me put the brakes on anything.

But the more time I spend with Millie, the more I can't stand to think of being with anyone else. It's like all the dates in my past are just some practice round to show me what I was missing out on in my life once Millie came into it.

We're swimming in the large pool. I'm passing the football for the boys to dive in and try to catch, and Millie is swimming close by.

"So, we've got about fifteen hours until the wedding. Is there anything you want to do before that happens?" I ask her. Frank throws the ball back to me, but it's short and water splashes all over my face. Once my eyes are finally clear, I turn to see a server trying to get my attention.

"The nachos are on that table right there. The other half of the order will be here in a few minutes, sir."

"Thank you," I say, taking a few steps through the water to collect the football. But the boys are swimming toward the nachos. Millie plants herself in front of the ladder to get out of the pool, blocking her brothers.

"Those aren't yours. You don't just take something Spencer ordered without asking first."

Frank and Eric turn to me. "Please, Spencer. Can we have some nachos?"

I laugh and nod. "Yeah, go for it."

Millie shakes her head. "You know they're going to eat it all, right?"

"I'm okay with that. I ordered it to share, anyway."

Mr. Olsen is walking across the deck with a little bag. "Are you good with the boys here?" he asks Millie.

"Did you get the medicine?" she asks in a sharp tone.

Her dad pulls out a bottle from the bag. "Is this what she needs?"

"Yeah, hurry and get it to her." She turns to me and I must've had a questioning look on my face because she says, "My mom has a migraine."

I clap my hands together, and Millie's eyes widen, looking confused. "Are you clapping that my mom is in pain?"

I drop my hands back into the water. "Of course not. I was clapping because you were assertive and got right to the point. I'm proud of you."

She gives me a small smile. "Thanks, teacher."

"I didn't do much," I say, laughing.

She uses the ladder to get out of the water, and I try to avoid watching her backside as she does so. I follow, handing her the extra towel I grabbed when I walked in.

"Boys, leave some for Spencer."

Danny, Frank, and Eric all freeze and sit back, their faces covered in cheese, sour cream, and guacamole.

"You're good. I only need a couple," I say, picking up a chip and biting into it. The server comes over with a small tray of mozzarella sticks and I thank him before holding the tray out to the boys. "Take one."

I reach the plate out to Millie with the last one there. "Here's our snack before dinner," I say with a smile.

She takes it and sits down in the chair next to me. The boys wipe off their faces and head to the pool again.

Millie lays back, closing her eyes and relaxing into the chair. She looks so relaxed and there's so much I want to say to her. I just don't know how she'll take it if I tell her I like her. I've never had this problem before. She's seen me with or heard of me taking out dozens of women over the past six months. And she totally called it. I was going out with the women who I thought were attractive, but had no other redeeming qualities to them. But Amelia Jane Olsen embodies both attractiveness and depth, kindness and loyalty.

Yep, I've definitely fallen for my best friend's sister.

40

SPENCER

I'm back in the room an hour later and my stomach has been grumbling ever since I ate that mozzarella stick.

Beau is tying a tie. "Are you all right? You don't look good."

"I don't feel good. I'm going to lie down for a minute. Maybe that'll help before we have to go downstairs."

"What did you do? Drink all the pool water?"

I think back to the time in the pool and shake my head. The boys had been wrestling with me in the water, but I didn't inhale as much as Frank did in our playing.

"No, I was just playing with your brothers and then ate some appetizers that I ordered for the group," I say, lying down on the bed again.

"Do you need a bowl or something? You're practically green." Beau takes another look at my face before he glances around the room, searching for something. "I think the best thing we have is the ice bucket."

I shake my head, hoping to ward off whatever is coming at me and then change my mind. "Yeah, maybe I should use that."

"Do you need me to get some medicine or anything?" Beau

hands me the bowl but leans back and then dances away from me. I get it. The poor guy gets married tomorrow. He doesn't want to go on his honeymoon with a virus.

"Maybe a soda or something."

He nods. "You got it. I'll go grab it right now."

I feel bad that I got sick right before dinner, but how am I supposed to control that? Then again, it might not be the worst thing. After a few hours of rest, I'll be ready for the wedding in the morning. Maybe.

By the time there's a knock at the door, I've given up my lunch at least three times. On wobbly legs, I make it to open the door, wondering why Beau wouldn't just use his key to get back in.

Instead, Millie is on the other side, holding a bag full of stuff, and she looks horrified.

"Are you all right?" she asks, closing the door while I stumble toward the bed again. My body is exhausted and all I want is sleep.

"Trying to be. It's not going well." I hug a pillow close to me, making sure the ice bucket is still within reach for easy access. Never have I wished more that I could be in my own home.

"Okay, I'm armed with a bit of everything." She sets the grocery bag on the bed and rifles through it, finally pulling out a bottle of Sprite and a few boxes of medicine. She walks around the bed to my side and reaches out to touch my fore-head. "You're burning up."

"W-w-w-hy is it s-s-s-o c-cold in here?" My body is all about the chills, and I wish it was solely because Millie is standing next to me. It is comforting that she came to check on me, though.

She undoes the bottle and hands it to me. The bubbles in the soda help settle the nausea just a tad, which is some relief.

"Take a few of these," Millie says, handing me a small clear cup filled with Pepto. She watches as I swallow it, as if she's a nurse making sure it all goes down.

"Do you have a room key here?" she asks. I'm already struggling to stay awake, so I motion to the dresser holding the TV and then close my eyes.

The door closes and then opens again. Warmth surrounds me and I peek my eyes open a bit to see Millie with the blanket we bought the first night of our road trip. That seems like so long ago and like it was yesterday.

"I'll be back to check on you," Millie says, leaning down and leaving a small kiss on my cheek. Somehow, that spot feels even hotter than the blaze my skin is already experiencing. The woman is amazing. I just need to get the strength to tell her that.

41

MILLIE

Leave it to Beau to freak out about his best man getting sick. He came over to our suite and made a big deal about not wanting to get sick the day before his honeymoon.

My mother asked if I would go get some stuff for Spencer, and because of the ask, I was a lot more willing to comply. Then again, it's for Spencer, so I would've done it anyway.

The dress rehearsal is probably the most boring thing ever. As the wedding director walks everyone through what will happen tomorrow morning, the number of times he says something about the best man keeps my thoughts on Spencer.

We finally get to the dinner portion, and I hurry to finish my food, wanting to go check on him, which is lucky because Trina's father has a microphone in hand and is already droning on about Trina's life since the toddler stage.

I head up the stairs and use the keycard from earlier to get into the room. It's dark and I have to wait a moment for my eyes to adjust. Spencer doesn't look like he's moved since I left, which makes me nervous that maybe he's suffocated or something.

I'm at the bed in two strides, tugging him from his side to his back. "Spencer, are you all right?"

All he gives me is a groan.

I turn on the bedside lamp, and he flinches, turning away from it. "Come on, you're not a vampire. How are you feeling?"

His complexion is white, but he gives me a thin smile. "I'm alive. No blood, please."

I chuckle at the vampire joke and work to adjust the blanket around him. "Do you need more pop? Medicine?"

The way his head flops from side to side in his answer has me wondering if he's all right. I pick up the small bottle of pink medicine and notice it's half gone.

"Did you drink this?"

"Yep," he says.

"Are you feeling okay?"

"You know, I'd like to kiss you, but not right now. I wouldn't want you to get sick." His words are slurred and I'm wondering if he's hallucinating.

"I'd rather I didn't get sick either, but I'll take a raincheck on the kissing part."

His eyebrows raise to his hairline and he says, "Really? You'd want to kiss me?'

Laughing, I say, "Absolutely. How about you rest right now and we can work on that tomorrow, if you're feeling better?"

"I like your thinking." He closes his eyes and I move to stand, but he reaches out and touches my hand. "Don't go."

There's an urge to leave the illness-infested air, but I also want to be here, to make sure Spencer has anything he might need.

"I'll lay on Beau's bed for a bit, and then I have to get down to dinner."

I turn on a movie, hoping to help even out the pitter patter of my heart from what I can only imagine will be a fantasy tomorrow. There's no way Spencer meant he wanted to kiss me, right?

My phone buzzes and I turn it over to see my father's name on the screen. Oh boy.

"Hey Dad," I say, making sure my tone is relaxed.

"Where are you?" His frustrated tone causes my stomach to tighten, like I've done something terribly wrong.

"I'm checking on Spencer."

There's a pause and then he says, "Are you done? We need to take some pictures, and your mother wants the whole family together."

I glance over at Spencer, who's now lightly snoring. "Yeah, I'll head back down."

After hanging up the phone, I glance over at Spencer again. "I'll be right back," I say softly, hoping he'll remember it even though he's sleeping soundly.

I make it back to the large room where most people have left, save my family and the smaller Burkhead clan.

My mother sees me and waves me over, her lips pinched. "Hurry. We've been waiting on you," she says.

"Why are we taking formal pictures at the rehearsal dinner? Isn't this something we should do tomorrow?" I say it loud enough that a few people overhear.

"Daphne wanted some of every moment. You can't keep sneaking off like that, especially tomorrow."

"Spencer is sick, Mom. I'm just trying to help him feel better."

The photographer organizes us and I'm sent to stand next to my father. At least I don't have to keep hearing the lecture my mother has for me.

We've taken at least a lifetime's worth of photos in five minutes and now I'm dreading everything about tomorrow. I'll probably end up with a wooden smile in the pictures because of the constant need to be ready to say cheese. At least Trina isn't an influencer or anything. I would hate to see the photos all over social media.

"Is Spencer going to be okay?" Trina asks after the group has been released.

"I hope so," I say. Because going to the wedding without a date might be worse than being the official babysitter to the Olsen family. The pitying looks from all the aunts and grandmas is something I don't need to round out this trip. Even if he's sick, they'll think it was because of something I did.

"Me too."

I don't know why I'm still surprised every time she speaks. Caring about someone who isn't Trina Burkhead is a definite miracle coming from her.

"Do you, uh, need anything before tomorrow?" I ask. I'm not the maid of honor, but as an olive branch that we really are moving in the right direction toward being friends, I figure helping as much as I can for this event can only be a good thing.

Trina gives me a big smile and shakes her head. "I think everything is set for now. Just be on time?"

I don't know why her saying it as a question makes me laugh, but I do. "Sorry, that just sounded funny. If anything, I'll be extra early. My mom is a little excited about this whole thing."

"At least yours is. Mine is not. But she hasn't made any comments today, so I'm calling it a win."

In a rash decision, I lean forward and pull Trina into a hug. She relaxes quite a bit and hugs me back. My mom is a lot of things, but I can't imagine her being awful about me getting married. If anything, I could see her giving away everything she owns just to see me marry someone.

I pull back a bit and say, "Tomorrow, you're going to have an amazing day. You'll be beautiful, as always, and you'll walk down the aisle to my brother—" I make a disgusted face, which causes her to laugh before I continue, "—and you'll be married and get to make your own family. You'll remember how you felt and then you'll make sure that your daughter doesn't have to feel that way, ever."

Trina's eyes fill with tears and she hugs me again, this time to the point I might run out of air. "Thank you again, Millie. You really are an amazing person. I wish I'd taken the time to figure that out sooner."

As I head back to my room, I can't help but have a bounce in my step. I'd been able to get over my hurt and anger in order to help Trina feel better. It's something that would've only happened in a nightmare before, but because of being here and learning from Spencer, I might actually enjoy having a sister-in-law.

42

SPENCER

"You should ask her out," Beau says, focusing on his image in the mirror as he fixes several things.

I survived Barf-aggedon last night and woke up sore, but much better. Sounds like I didn't miss much from the rehearsal dinner the night before. At least Millie took care of me, which is all I really care about.

"Who?" His comment catches me off guard and I try to figure out his line of thinking. I woke up feeling mostly like myself, aside from a haze around my memories.

"Millie."

"I already did. She's my date to your wedding, remember?" I say, trying to cover up how much I really want to do more than have one "official" date with her.

Beau walks over and puts his hand on my shoulder, looking me in the eyes. "I've seen you with her. You should go on a date."

I laugh, thinking that I'd never hear him say that. "You'd be okay with me dating your sister?"

"Is it something you actually want to do? Wait—you said dating? Like not a single date?"

"Beau, I feel like we've been on at least a handful of dates over the past ten days. And every time I see her, I want more time with her. And every time she's not around, I'm thinking about her."

With a chuckle, Beau pats me on the back and says, "Sounds about right, Spence. That's how I feel about Trina. I never thought it would happen, but it's like every other woman pales in comparison."

That's the right way to put it.

"Just to be clear, you're not mad?" I ask, not sure I can trust my hearing right now. "That I want to date your sister?"

"Are you kidding? I know you, man. I know you'll take care of her and that you'll do anything you can for her. She'll do the same for you."

Hope blooms in my chest and my brain goes through all the options of proper dates I can take her on. Then again, I've enjoyed the simple times just getting to know her, to see the wonderful, caring person she is.

I hop in the shower, grateful to have whatever sickness behind me. Once I'm out, Beau hands me a piece of paper.

"Hey, I guess your mom has been trying to reach you the past couple of days. Is your phone not working?"

I run my hand through my hair, trying to get some of the water out of it as I walk over to pick up my phone. The Do Not Disturb symbol is at the top. When did I turn that on? I click on past calls and realize I haven't received calls or texts for a few days.

Fixing the controls, I call my mom. "Hey Mom."

"You're alive," she says in a relieved voice. "I was lucky that I'd saved Beau's phone number."

"Sorry, I got a stomach bug and have been unresponsive for a bit. What's up?"

"When I got the mail a couple days ago, there was a letter forwarded to us with your name on it. I promise I rarely open your mail, but it was for an award ceremony and when I couldn't reach you, I opened it. You've been invited to accept an award."

"What award?" I ask. I haven't done a lot business-wise in the last year that would've received any accolades.

"It's a humanitarian thing from the Brighter Days Foundation. And the ceremony is tomorrow night." I worked hard to find the very best managers for the foundation I set up, and they've taken over the reins the past few months while I've been working on the podcast.

I grin. "That's great, Mom. I'll have to let them know about it so someone can go."

"Don't you want to be there? It's something you've worked so hard on."

Her words make me pause. "I don't know if I can make it back that quickly."

"You can take a flight and be here in time."

I sit down on the bed, trying to wrestle with the idea of it. Yeah, I could take a flight, which is my normal way to get places. But I'd be lying if I didn't say I was kind of looking forward to driving back to Boston with Millie.

"Let me think about it and I'll let you know."

"Sounds good. Your dad and I are so proud of you."

"Thanks, Mom. I've got to get ready for this wedding now."

I hang up the phone and stare at the wall. It's been a long time since I've received an award for anything, and that was in the acting realm. With this being for my foundation, it's a different feeling because of all the work that has gone into organizing and helping the group to help with the growth in the underserved areas of Boston.

"Something bad happen?" Beau asks, finishing his hair.

I shake my head. "Brighter Days is receiving an award tomorrow night."

"That's awesome, Spence. Are you going to go?"

"I'm not sure. I mean, I'm all the way over here."

Beau gives me a side-eye look and then laughs. "Spencer, just because my sister doesn't like to fly, shouldn't mean you can't. I'm pretty sure she's going back to Boston, so you'll see her again there."

"Do you think she'll survive without someone to keep her awake that whole time?" I ask, still not wanting to commit to being away from her.

"She's done it several times, so I think she'll be okay."

I stand up, finding the tie to complete the tux I'm wearing. As I'm tying it, I weigh the options. Do I head back and receive the award and just hope that Millie will make it to Boston safely? Or do I hang out and drive back with her? Either way, I need to find time to tell her how I feel.

43

MILLIE

I t's finally the wedding day. My mom woke me up at six to get ready and I'm already wishing I could sleep for a week after everything we've tried to pack into the past few days.

We're sent to an enormous room in the hotel that turned out to be the Presidential Suite. It's big enough for the wedding party to get ready, and there are several ladies doing hair and makeup. That's a pleasant surprise. I thought I was going to have to come up with some way to do my hair and I'm not that talented in the creative updo department.

Trina walks over and says to me, "I've got your dress on a rack over there. It's been steamed and ready to go."

I give her a genuine smile and say, "Thanks for that."

"You're good. I know you were busy helping Spencer last night," Trina says, giving me a wink. She then talks to the hairdresser behind my seat and says, "Make sure her hair is up."

The hairdresser works with my hair, twisting and pinning it all over my head. My hair is long, but I didn't realize it would take that much work to pin it all up in the back. By the time she's done, my head feels very heavy.

"You look beautiful," my mom says, walking over to where I'm just getting finished with makeup.

"You too, Mom," I say. I don't think I've ever seen her with her hair done differently, but now it's pulled back in a sleek chignon and she's got a light touch of makeup, which she doesn't wear at home.

"Let me help you get your dress on." It takes some work, but we do it without pulling out any of the pins and beads the woman stuck in my hair. The short heels won't be comfortable to wear all day, so I sneak on a pair of flip-flops for now.

There's a small selection of drinks on a table at the other end of the room, along with a few small snacks. I walk over and pick up an orange juice, needing it to soothe my throat after the long night. Hopefully I'm not coming down with a bug like Spencer. It's then that I see Elaine walk in wearing the lacy cream dress she'd tried on at the boutique.

I'm standing in the corner, where I have a full view of the situation. When Trina turns around, her expression morphs into one of horror.

"What are you wearing, Elaine? I thought you were going to wear the rose-colored one we picked out."

"This one fits me better."

I don't think I've ever seen Trina so vulnerable, but now it's clear she doesn't have the support I always thought she would.

"You can't wear that."

"It's fine. Now, if I never find a husband, at least I'll have the experience of wearing white to a wedding."

"Join a dating app or plan a party where you pretend to get married. Just don't do it today."

I can see that Elaine isn't even considering it. After scanning the room for Mrs. Burkhead, I can see she's getting her hair done in a far chair. Was she behind this? I hadn't seen much of her relationship with her younger daughter, but would she really want to sabotage her elder daughter's wedding that badly?

Trina is near tears, looking as though she's not sure what to do about the situation.

I take a sip of my orange juice and make a decision. With glass in hand, I walk over near Elaine and "trip" on her train, throwing my orange juice all over the side of her in the process.

"I'm so sorry," I say, doing my best to make it believable. I grab a napkin from the table and dab at the orange, which only makes it set into the fabric a little more.

"How dare you!" Elaine shouts before she slaps me on the cheek. She's screaming at me, saying all these things about me being from a backwoods family and how her sister shouldn't have stooped so low as to even consider marrying my brother.

"Get out," Trina says to Elaine, firmly.

"Mom and Dad are paying for this wedding, Trina. You can't kick me out."

Trina shakes her head and says, "I'll get married in a tent if I have to. I'm done with this."

My mom guides me to a chair and lightly touches my cheek. She says, "It's a little red. Are you okay?"

I give her a small smile. "Yeah, it was worth it."

My mom searches my face for something and then reaches over and pulls me in for a hug. "I'm so proud of you, darling."

I nod toward Trina's mom and sister before I say, "As long as we don't get like that, I think we'll be okay."

The large doors open and two men walk toward Elaine, ushering her out of the room. Mrs. Burkhead follows, her hair half-done as she screeches something. At least the closed door masks some of it.

It's only then that I realize Trina is standing in front of me. "Thank you for what you did."

"No problem. I figured you wouldn't want to deal with that all day."

"I'm sorry for what she said. To be honest, your family has been nothing but kind to me since I started hanging out with Beau. I hope you don't think I feel the same way as my sister."

"What's family for?" I say with a smile.

"There's a vacancy for maid of honor? Do you mind filling it for me?" Trina asks, her expression hopeful.

I smile and laugh a little, wondering how within the span of a week, I went from thinking this woman was my enemy to now being her right-hand gal in her wedding. "I'd love to."

44

SPENCER

"Are you ready for this?" I ask Beau, straightening his tie and helping him with his collar that was sticking up. It had been fine in the room, but even he seems nervous and keeps messing with everything while we wait in the hallway.

He nods, giving me a small smile. "Yeah, I'm ready."

"What about after the honeymoon? Where are you going to live?"

"Probably here in Danton, or wherever we decide to be."

"And you're okay with that?"

He looks at me this time and says, "It's not Boston, but if that's what's going to make my Trina happy, then it's worth it."

I lean in. "Who are you, and what have you done with Beau Olsen?"

He laughs and says, "Well, I've had to think about a lot the past few days. Trina's been through so much with her family and this wedding. The least I can do is help her be happy."

I squeeze his shoulder and nod. There's nothing I wanted more than to see him caring about someone else.

"As far as the podcast and the voice platform, if you'll send me some papers, I'll sign everything over to you. You've done the most work on them and I don't want you to worry about it since I won't be heading back east soon."

That makes me smile. He's tying up loose ends and letting me know his plans for the future.

That means a lot to me.

I glance out over the crowd and see Scotty Duncan there in the third row back. He gives me a small smile and I turn to focus on the doors. I don't need to ruin a pleasant moment by the past.

The doors open, and the bridesmaids start down the aisle. There's one I can't take my gaze from. She's the last one down the aisle with her red hair pulled back and the dress accentuating every curve. Wait, why is she in the maid of honor spot?

I can't help but grin at her and she gives me a shy smile back. Millie lines up on the other side of the aisle with the rest of the bridesmaids and I'm wishing we could stand next to each other and say vows like this.

That's when my brain is going into overdrive, wondering why the jump from crush to wanting to get married. I've always run away from the idea of marriage, commitment even. And here I am, wishing Millie felt the same way about me as I do about her.

Trina walks out with her arm looped through Beau's dad's arm. There is confusion throughout the crowd, but Trina looks calm and more relaxed than I've seen her since we met at the campground.

"What happened?" I try to ask Beau discreetly. Scanning the attendees, there's no sign of Mr. and Mrs. Burkhead or Elaine.

Beau shakes his head. "I don't know."

Once they make it to the front and the preacher says the line about who will give the bride away, Beau's dad says, "I do."

Beau takes Trina's hand to help her up the few steps on the

platform and I hear him whisper, "Are you okay? What happened?"

She smiles at him and says, "It's a story for later. Let's get married."

They say their vows and the newlyweds make it down the aisle to cheers, mostly from the groom's family.

I walk over to Millie and hold out my arm for her. "I see you've been promoted."

"Yeah, it's been quite the morning." She quickly fills me in on Elaine trying to upstage Trina and her mother supporting her in it.

"You really spilled orange juice all over the dress?" When Millie blushes and nods, I hold out my hand for a high-five. "That's the best thing I've heard all week."

"You look like you feel better. I'm glad you're here."

That's when my brain remembers about the humanitarian award. "I got some news this morning. The foundation I started a few years ago is getting an award for all the work we've done the past year."

"That's so great. When is the ceremony?"

I give her a sad smile and say, "Tomorrow night."

"Are you going? You should." Millie stops and turns to me, grinning.

"I'd have to fly out tonight or early tomorrow morning to make it." I pause, waiting for her reaction.

She nods. "That's usually how flights work. Go. You should celebrate such an award."

"Will you be okay driving back by yourself?" I ask, secretly wanting her to say no and that she needs me there with her.

Instead, she nods and says, "Of course. I'll just load up on Dr. Pepper and sunflower seeds. But this time, I promise to reserve a hotel room before I stop."

"How about you let me book those for you," I say with a

laugh. Why I'm feeling so down about this whole thing, I'm not sure. I'll see her in Boston in a matter of days.

"Deal. Okay, I've got a few things to check on, now that I've been promoted to maid of honor, but I'll see you later?"

I nod, leaning down and kissing her cheek. She grins at me and squeezes my hand before walking away.

It's official. I've lost my heart to my best friend's sister.

It's then that I focus on the guy standing in the doorway she leaves through. Scotty.

I turn to walk away, knowing I'm being the coward right now.

"Spencer, stop. We need to talk." I can hear his footsteps coming up behind me and I finally stop.

"Why do you want to talk now? When you could've reached out for the past ten years?" My chest constricts as the pain of those memories crops up.

"Spencer, you looked at me like I was perfect. You used to imitate me from my clothes all the way to how I talked. I knew that if you found out how much I was struggling with my addiction, that you'd never look at me the same. Being immature and nineteen, I figured I'd hurt you less if I just left."

I try to picture myself at nineteen. Sure, the decisions weren't always sound back then, but I tried to make up for any mistakes I made.

"But you kept talking to my parents. Why—"

"They told me I needed to talk to you, but I just kept saying I couldn't do it. As the months and years passed, it was harder and harder to know how to explain everything."

I shrug, trying to make it look like all this doesn't affect me this much. "So, if you hadn't been related to the bride of the wedding I would be at, I still wouldn't have heard from you?"

Scotty blows out a breath and says, "I actually called your dad the other day, and he said you were heading to a wedding out here. We connected the dots, and I knew it was time to apologize."

"I needed you, Scotty."

"Is that why you quit acting? Because I left?" he asks.

"My heart wasn't in it anymore. And the parts changed. I needed a change." I've never really put all that together before this, but I'd blamed Scotty's departure for hurting my life, when it actually just helped in the aging process.

"I promise, I never meant to hurt you. My only intention was to save you from the shame of being my friend."

Shaking my head, I say, "It takes a lot for me to get rid of friends, no matter what they do."

Scotty slaps me on the shoulder and says, "I've missed you, brother. I hope you know that."

He gets emotional, which only causes my throat to close up. I'm transported to who I was at sixteen and those weeks and months of worry and not knowing what happened.

"I do. I missed you too." We hug and I breathe in, feeling like a weight has been lifted from my chest.

"I hear you're getting an award. Congratulations," Scotty says, smiling widely. "You better check the weather and get on a plane soon. Do you mind if we catch up more the next time I'm in Boston?"

"Absolutely. If you're willing, I'd love to have you as a guest on a podcast I'm working on."

"That I can do."

I head out, grateful for the chance to learn the truth, and for the hope of what the future will bring.

45

MILLIE

I've gone through everything, making sure the reception dinner will go off without a hitch.

Trina hugs me tightly once she comes into the reception hall. "You're amazing, you know that, right? I don't think I could've made it through this day without you and Beau. And your family."

"Are you sure you're talking about the right family?" I say with a laugh. As frustrated as I had been with them before coming home, I love them all much more now. It took me nearly twenty-three years to put my foot down, and for the most part, they've respected my opinions.

My dad walked Trina down the aisle and then my mother did everything she could to make Trina feel better when it came time for family pictures after the ceremony.

"Where's Spencer?" Trina asks, looking around the room.

Beau walks up just then and says, "He took my car to get to the airport. We'll have someone pick it up later."

He found me when I was fixing the centerpieces on the tables for the reception. Because of a storm coming in tomorrow, he'd booked a ticket for this evening. And he'd been able to talk to Scotty Duncan, which makes it seem like miracles are happening for both of us in this small town.

"You didn't go with him?" Trina asks, staring at me with a half-smile.

I shake my head. "No, I don't do well on planes and he'd miss the whole thing even if we started driving tonight."

"What don't you like about them?" Trina asks.

"This is your wedding reception. We can talk all about my weird quirks later," I say, glancing around as the room fills with people.

"Millie, do you like him?"

Her straightforward question has me doing a mental evaluation. But it should be more of the heart check, because I am definitely in the love category right now.

"Yes," I say, feeling the rightness of it spread through my body like a zap of electricity.

"Then go to him. Catch a flight and be there for him when he accepts the award." Trina's expression is so earnest that I get excited for a few moments before I remember that he probably doesn't like me.

"I can't. And I doubt he'd even want more than being friends with Beau's little sister. I'm like a love pariah." It hurts just to think about it like that.

"Come on, Millie," Beau says. "He likes you too. He was going to stay and miss the awards until you told him to go."

It takes several moments for my brain to register that fact. "Really?"

Beau and Trina nod in unison.

"Go pack and we'll get someone to drive you to the airport. Beau will book you a ticket and then you can tell us all about it after our honeymoon." Trina grins and it makes me wonder what our relationship could've been like in high school had she been more like this.

"But the reception. You've already lost your sister and parents—"

Trina holds up a hand. "We're already married. That's the most important part. You were here for the pictures. You don't need to sit here bored talking to people you don't know while you're wishing you were somewhere else."

Eric and Frank sneak up and start saying, "Spencer and Millie sittin' in a tree, K-I-S-S-I-N-G! First comes love—"

Beau drags them away and says, "I think that's enough, boys. Let's go see what treats we can sneak before the reception starts."

Trina gives me another hug and says, "You've been brave this entire trip. It's time to turn that up another notch and go get Spencer. Tell him how you feel."

It's like she's just shot a gun to start a race and I turn around, rushing toward the doors and up to the room. I throw everything I brought back into the suitcase and have to keep focusing on the fact that after a terrifying flight, I'll get to see Spencer. Tell him how I feel.

That's going to need some practice, but I've got a few hours to figure out my speech.

There's a knock on the door just as I'm zipping up the duffle bag. I open the door to see my dad.

"I heard you need a ride."

46

MILLIE

That I'm in shock is putting it mildly. "Um, yeah."

"I thought you were scared of flying."

I nod. "Yeah, I definitely am."

He nods, tucking his hand into the pocket of his suit pants. "So, is there any reason you're okay with going now and not when we needed you to come out?"

I've never talked to my father about the mundane parts of my life regularly, let alone any romantic pursuits. But I say, "I think I love Spencer."

There's a flash of surprise in his eyes and then a smile. "Well, that explains a lot. Are you ready to go?"

"Aren't you needed down at the reception?"

"Your mother gave me a pass. We did most of the bigger stuff at dinner last night, and she figured this would be a good time to chat before you head back to your exciting life in Boston."

Leave it to my mother to keep surprising me on this trip.

We head down to the truck and drive the hour to get to the nearest airport. My dad doesn't say much until we're just a few minutes away.

"You know, I didn't realize how strong you are as a person. I'm sorry that I never gave you the chance to show me before." He cuts off and it looks like my dad, the toughest and most stoic person I've ever known, is getting choked up. "I'm proud of you. So proud."

He stops the truck next to the departure door and puts it into park. I lean over and give him a hug. "Thanks, Dad. That means a lot."

"I've transferred the money to your account. Thank you for being here. Good luck with Spencer. Maybe you'll have your own wedding bells happening soon."

Laughing, I say, "We can only hope." I jump out of the truck and grab my bag. It's only after I've gotten my boarding pass that I see I'll be in a little puddle jumper plane to another airport until a bigger flight takes off late tonight. I'll have red eyes by the end of this adventure, but hopefully I can get the guy.

47

SPENCER

I've been debating whether it was a good thing to fly out since I got on the first plane to my connecting flight. Should I have left? Or will Millie actually miss me now that I've left? I guess this will test the "absence makes the heart grow fonder" theory.

I end up in Boston around six the next morning and take an Uber home. My body is heavy with exhaustion because sleeping on planes isn't something I'm great at. Before I lay down for a nap, I send Millie a quick text.

Me: Hey! When are you starting your journey back to Boston?

I wait a few moments, but then realize that she's in a time-zone two hours behind me.

Me: I just got in and I'm going to take a nap. Let me know and maybe I'll fly somewhere to meet up with you.

I sleep soundly, which happens in my own bed, with the pillows, sheets and blankets I'm used to. But I wouldn't trade the road trip experience with Millie for the world.

I'm woken up by a knock on my door. Actually, it's more of a pounding and I drag myself out of bed, glancing at the clock on the wall that says it's three o'clock. In the afternoon? I've never slept that long before.

My mother is standing on the other side of the door, and she rushes in to give me a hug. "You made it back. Oh, it's so good to see you."

I chuckle and say, "I've only been gone for a few days, Mom."

"Well, I missed you. How was the wedding?" She walks into the front room and lays a dry-cleaning bag on the couch before sitting down.

"It was good. I missed the reception to fly back, but everything else was fun. Definitely a lot of learning for me."

"I'm glad you made it back safely. How was the road trip with Millie?"

My brain takes me back to all the adventures we'd been through on the short trip, and I can't help but smile. "It was great. Her family is a little quirky, but I think Millie sees them in a different light. She's great."

"That's good to hear. She's a lovely girl."

With a nod, I say, "That she is."

"Okay, well, I picked up your suit yesterday and had the dry cleaners do a rush on it. Have you thought about an acceptance speech yet?"

I hadn't gotten that far. My thoughts have been so tangled up with the woman I left back in Colorado that I'm feeling even more guilty I didn't just stay with her.

"No."

"We've got time to work on it. Why don't you change and then we'll head back to the house. We can get you all ready for the big night."

I'm here. I might as well make the best of it.

My phone is sitting on my nightstand and I pick it up, hoping to see a message from Millie. There's nothing there.

Maybe she's caught up in the after-wedding clean-up? I just

hope she can keep holding her own, and making sure she takes up the space she deserves.

Me: I hope you slept well. Call me when you get a chance.

I pack a few things and bring my phone charger, since I forgot to charge it when I got home. It's funny how much a phone has been a critical part of my relationship with Millie. Hopefully, she didn't lose hers. I'm itching to talk to her again, to hear her thoughts on how the rest of the night went. And to tell her I love her.

I laugh, wondering how that cropped up so quickly. It's not possible to fall in love with someone in a week, is it?

Then again, I can see little instances that helped me on that journey. I've been drawn to her long before Beau left and it's only in hindsight that I can register why.

The next few hours go by quickly and the sky opens up and downpours as we drive to the convention center. My mother is the queen of preparedness and hands me an umbrella when we get out. The dinner is only about a block from the parking garage, but I feel a chill as I walk into the large room set out with circular tables. It looks a lot like the reception I ditched yesterday.

I recognize several people from other foundations and am grateful to my mother, who invited the people in my organization who are on the ground daily, checking in on all the aspects and events that we work on throughout the year.

The program starts, and I'm trying to be content with the fact that Millie hasn't texted me yet.

Instead, I get a text from Beau.

Beau: Congrats on the award, man. Where are they holding the ceremony?

Me: Shouldn't you be on your honeymoon?

Beau: We're heading there. But I wanted to thank you for coming out.

I text him once more before tucking the phone back into my coat pocket, knowing I need to be present for this.

They've announced and awarded several other foundations. The last award is for the Brighter Days Foundation.

I walk to the stage with my team, wishing Millie were here. Just to have her there to celebrate with me. At least my parents made it.

We're given a large glass trophy and the team waves me up to the microphone.

"I just want to thank you all for your support of Brighter Days. It's a project I started at a point when I had no idea what to do with my life after acting. It helped me to look outside myself, to see the challenges of those around me." I smile over at my parents and say, "Thank you to my parents, for pushing me to find a way to serve others. To say I have an amazing team to accomplish all that would be an understatement. Because of these people behind me, we've been able to help thousands of children in Massachusetts get the food, clothing, school supplies and tutoring they need to be successful in life."

It's then that I see a familiar figure in the back of the room. Millie is drenched from head to toe from the rain outside, but I can see her beaming up at me.

I hand the microphone off to one of my assistants and try to be patient as the thank yous are wrapped up for our award. As soon as I can, I hurry off the stage and make my way through the tables, with so many eyes watching me. My sights are set on the woman I've fallen in love with.

Wanting a private moment, I take her hand and tug her gently toward the door. "What are you doing here?" I say, pulling her to me. "How did you even get here?"

"I flew," she says, laughing.

I lean back so I can see her face. "You flew?"

"We got delayed and then rerouted and I don't know if

being in an airplane or an airport for the past eighteen hours has cured me of my fears, but I'm just glad I'm here."

I take off my coat and tug it around her, hoping to ward off the chill from the hallway. The rain is still coming down outside.

"What made you get on a plane in the first place?"

"You," she says, with a soft smile. "I wanted to say that I think I'm falling for you. And—"

Before she can say anything else, I lean down and kiss her. She's stiff at first and then she seems to relax, as if understanding what this is all about. I pull her closer, kissing her for several moments before pulling away.

"Sorry, I didn't let you finish. What were you going to say?" I ask, with a chuckle.

Millie laughs and says, "I was going to say that I think I've liked you since before we left on our road trip, but I didn't realize it fully until we danced. And then I just wanted to kiss you, but now you're my first kiss and I was worried I'd be horrible at it—"

"For the record, I wouldn't have noticed it was your first time. But I'm always game to practice. Practice is something I'm great at," I say, grinning.

We kiss again, and it's like sharing everything we've gone through over the past couple of weeks. The highs, the lows, and the times we've just been together.

We pull back and stand there, embracing for another few minutes. "I can't believe you got on a plane for me."

"You taught me to conquer a few of my fears. I figured it was time to get over one more so I could be here for you tonight. Sorry that I look like a drowned cat, though."

I gently tilt her head up and say, "You look just as beautiful as you always do. What do you say we head out?"

"What about the awards?" she asks, pointing to the closed door.

"They're almost over, anyway. Let's go get some food."

"Takeout and then a movie night?" she asks hopefully.

"As long as you're there, it sounds like an absolutely perfect night."

Millie stops me when we're close to the door and says, "I was going to show you something." She hurries over to her suitcase that's up against the wall. With her phone in her hands, she taps away at it. When she's next to me, she says, "I was on a layover and couldn't sleep last night. I figured you'd probably still be flying at that point, but look what I found."

She turns the phone around so I can see the screen. I recognize the colors and font from the Love, Austen app.

Raising an eyebrow, I say, "Um, did your ghost date finally contact you?"

Millie looks confused and turns to see that the app must've kicked her out. She logs in and then hits the home button. There on the screen is my profile picture.

"Did you log into my account on your phone?"

She laughs and says, "No. Spencer, this is my top three matches. Ghost Boy is no longer on here but look who is." She's pointing at my picture.

I grin and say, "For real? Had I known I'd match with you, I would've filled out that ridiculous questionnaire a long time ago."

"I don't know if it would've made a difference. At least you didn't run away when you saw how dysfunctional my family is."

"We all have quirks. As long as you're okay with mine, we'll get along just fine."

I lean in to kiss her again. It's short and sweet before I pull back, reveling in the moment. My life has twisted and turned in so many directions that I didn't think were for a good reason. And yet, here I am, at the start of something great with a wonderful woman in front of me.

"So, where are we on the relationship scale?" Millie asks with a grin. "Friend zone?"

"I'm ready to tell everyone you're my girlfriend. Are you good with that?"

Millie grins before leaning up on her tiptoes to kiss me again. "It's my dream come true."

EPILOGUE
SPENCER

3 months later

I'm nervous. I shouldn't be, but the box in my pocket is making me second-guess everything right now. Is it too soon to propose to Millie?

It's been a busy summer, even if it's only July. Millie and I have been together ever since the road trip, seeing each other daily. I would love nothing more than to say vows with her standing next to me. I kept thinking that at Evie and Owen's wedding, which was only two weeks after the Olsen-Burkhead wedding.

Now we're at our favorite pizza place in a back room for a goodbye party. Not for us. Kenzie and Trey got married three weeks ago, and are preparing to move to Utah, where he's been traded to play hockey for the Utah Yetis. They got word about it just a few days before the wedding. They'll be missed, but it also gives us an excuse to head out and visit. And enjoy the few times his team will come and play the Breeze.

Beau and Trina moved to Boston two weeks ago. After their honeymoon, things didn't go well with her family, and she told

Beau that he didn't have to work for her family if he didn't want to. I happily took him back and he's been more involved than ever in helping with our businesses, probably because there's someone else depending on him now.

Millie has been stressed the past couple of weeks as she worked to get caught up on her schoolwork and finals. But she's been able to use some of her skills to help us with the backend of the podcast, keeping me in check when I want to spend crazy amounts of money on random things that won't benefit the growth of the business.

Kenzie and Trey walk in, and I can tell it's going to be an emotional night from the way her eyes are red-rimmed. Our group has been amazing for the past two years, and it's hard to see a piece of them not be around anymore.

The rest of the group trickles in, everyone hugging Kenzie and Trey.

We order pizza and chat around the tables. Once everyone finishes eating, Trey stands up, tapping his fork against his soda glass. The room quiets down and he gives us all a smile, not as big as is usual for him.

"Thanks for coming, guys and gals. We love every one of you. You've all been instrumental in our lives here in Boston. Thanks to all the guys for their support and for being the best friends a guy can ask for. And to the ladies, thanks for taking care of Kenzie for the past two years."

"Here, here!" Dani says, holding up her glass. Miles scoots his chair back in anticipation of the spillage, which is apparently just another part of their story.

"We've loved Boston and everything about it, but we're starting a new chapter in Utah. I have two things to propose: First, that we organize and plan a friend reunion yearly, preferably in the summer so the two of us can make it," he says with a wink.

"I love that idea," Evie says, gushing next to Millie.

"Aww," Rachelle says. "Then our kids can all grow up knowing one another." That makes the entire group of ladies ooh and ahh.

"Are we still invited if we're single?" Jack asks from the end of the table.

"I don't think you'll be single for long," Owen says, glancing between Hillary and Jack.

Evie elbows him and he doubles over, laughing as quietly as possible. That only causes a chain reaction of laughter at the table.

"What's the second proposal?" Millie asks, looking over at Trey. With her back turned to me, I try to slide out my chair as quietly as possible. I sink down to a kneeling position, only to hear a loud rip. Were those my pants?

All eyes turn to me and I try to smile, hoping Millie will say yes.

"Um, that proposal was my assignment, uhm, request. Amelia Jane Olsen, I know it's soon—"

"Not soon enough!" Hillary says from behind me. The room laughs quickly and then settles down, as if we're the major movie after all the previews.

"But we've done so much in the last few months and you still don't mind hanging out with me," I say with a chuckle. Millie has her hand over her mouth and her eyes wide. Hopefully she's still breathing.

"Will you make me the happiest man ever—"

"Too late," Miles says, leaning over to kiss Dani.

"I repeat, the happiest man ever and be my wife?" There it is. That millisecond where I'm not sure if she's going to say yes or no.

Then she nods, and grins through tears. "Yes, so many times, yes." She lunges toward me, so I don't even have a chance to open the ring box.

"Take the PDA outside!" Jack says, and I can only smile as I kiss Millie.

We split apart and sit down, allowing Trey to continue his goodbye sermon. I pull the ring out of the box and slip it onto her finger. It was the second biggest diamond they had ready at the jewelers when I went looking yesterday.

"How long have you been planning this?" Millie whispers.

"Remember the trip I took for the foundation last week?" She nods and I say, "I took a detour on the way back to talk to your mom and dad about it."

Her eyes go wide again and she says, "You didn't."

Nodding, I say, "I did. And they were fully onboard. I even told your brothers and Frank gave me ideas on how to propose with mud."

She laughs. "I'm glad you didn't use that idea. Even though I love the kid."

After we all say our goodbyes, I walk with Millie to the parking garage, where I left my car.

"I love you, Millie."

"I love you too, Spencer." She leans up on her tiptoes and we kiss softly. I still can't believe this woman is going to be my wife.

"How about another road trip soon?"

She laughs and says, "Only if I can drive."

ACKNOWLEDGMENTS

It's been a while since I've released a book, but there are some great people I need to thank. Without them, this book would probably sit as a draft on my computer.

Thanks to Nina for her work in helping me craft the best story and the best characters. I am so grateful you reached out to help me when I needed it.

Thank you to Sheree Bingham, who constantly checks on me to make sure I'm reaching my deadlines. I always need that nudge, especially trying to write during the summer.

Thanks to my beta readers. You all put up with a rough storyline and helped to give me insight into where I needed to change things. Thank you a million for your help.

To my husband and family, who've survived my writing at odd hours of the day. Thanks for being my ultimate support system.

And to anyone else I might've forgotten, know that I'll figure it out in the middle of the night :)

ALSO BY BRITNEY M. MILLS

Romance by Love, Austen

Matched with Her Runaway Groom

Matched with Her Fake Fiancé

Matched with Her Athlete Boss

Matched with the Boy Next Door

Love Austen Series

Love, Austen

Austen, Party of Two

Austen Unscripted

Matched, Austen

Austen, Edited

Testing Love, Austen

International Billionaire Club

The Australian Billionaire

The French Billionaire

The British Billionaire

The Vegas Billionaire

The Italian Billionaire

Christmas at Coldwater Creek

Love in a Blizzard

Love in the Lights

Love in a Snapshot

Love in the Details

Rosemont High Baseball

The Perfect Play

The Perfect Game

The Perfect Catch

The Perfect Steal

The Perfect Hit

Sage Creek Small Town Series

Loving His Flower Shop Girl

Loving His Reporter Girl

Subscribe to the newsletter to get updates on books coming out, cover reveals and the opportunity for giveaways!

ABOUT THE AUTHOR

By day, Britney M. Mills is the wife to a builder and mom to five, but by night, she turns into an author, writing YA & contemporary romance stories.

A book lover, former college athlete, and Jane Austen fan, she crafts stories with the idea that anyone can find love.

When she's not writing, she spends time playing games with her kids, or shuttling them to and from their activities, watching Sanditon and Murdock Mysteries, or dreaming of future characters while she folds a mountain of laundry.

Subscribe to Britney's newsletter for updates, behind-the-scenes and a free book to dive into today!

www.ingramcontent.com/pod-product-compliance
Lightning Source LLC
Chambersburg PA
CBHW030106260626
47156CB00008B/2540

* 9 7 8 1 9 5 4 2 3 7 5 3 7 *